FINN

AND THE
SUBATOMIC
SLIP-AND-SLIDE

ALSO BY MICHAEL BUCKLEY

The Sisters Grimm series

The NERDS series

Finn and the Intergalactic Lunchbox

Finn and the Time-Traveling Pajamas

FINN
and the
SUBATOMIC
SLIP-and-SLIDE

MICHAEL BUCKLEY

DELACORTE PRESS

Text copyright © 2022 by Michael Buckley
Jacket art copyright © 2022 by Petur Antonsson

All rights reserved. Published in the United States by Delacorte Press, an imprint of Random House Children's Books, a division of Penguin Random House LLC, New York.

Delacorte Press is a registered trademark and the colophon is a trademark of Penguin Random House LLC.

Visit us on the Web! rhcbooks.com

Educators and librarians, for a variety of teaching tools, visit us at RHTeachersLibrarians.com

Library of Congress Cataloging-in-Publication Data
Names: Buckley, Michael, author.
Title: Finn and the subatomic slip and slide / Michael Buckley.
Description: First edition. | New York : Delacorte Press, [2022] | Series: The Finniverse ; book 3 | Audience: Ages 10 and up. | Summary: Finn and his friends travel to the subatomic, a microscopic world where Finn hopes to find his father and defeat the Plague once and for all.
Identifiers: LCCN 2020054098 (print) | LCCN 2020054099 (ebook) | ISBN 978-0-525-64695-2 (hardcover) | ISBN 978-0-525-64697-6 (library binding) | ISBN 978-0-525-64696-9 (ebook)
Subjects: CYAC: Space and time—Fiction. | Adventure and adventurers—Fiction. | Extraterrestrial beings—Fiction. | Friendship—Fiction. | Science fiction.
Classification: LCC PZ7.B882323 Fir 2022 (print) | LCC PZ7.B882323 (ebook) | DDC [Fic]—dc23

The text of this book is set in 11.25-point New Century Schoolbook LT Pro.

Printed in the United States of America
10 9 8 7 6 5 4 3 2 1
First Edition

For Imogen Miller

"**A**re you trying to get yourself killed, Julep?" Truman complained through her earpiece.

"You are very grouchy tonight," she teased. Her brother was the worrier, always scolding her to work faster, demanding she be more alert, get the job done, and go. She was the risk-taker who enjoyed the missions and didn't hide it. She knew it drove him crazy.

"I'm grouchy because you don't take this seriously," he said.

"I take it very seriously," she replied as she slinked through the shadows beneath the Plague watchtower. It was two stories tall, with a searchlight that scanned the neighborhood for human activity. She was careful not to step into the light and set off alarms. "Have you forgotten I have four successful sabotage missions under my belt this week? I'm causing a heap of headaches for the bugs. By the way, you're supposed to use my code name."

"Fine, Mongoose! You have been successful, but you've nearly gotten caught all four times," he cried. "It's almost shift change. Fresh guards are—"

"—alert guards. Yeah, yeah. And how many times do I have to tell you? It's *the* Mongoose!"

"Whatever. Just hurry."

"You can see I'm going as fast as I can." She glanced at the tree line and waved to the red lights hidden in the branches. It was her brother's drone, following close behind like it did on every mission.

Truman grumbled.

She laughed and went back to work. Tonight on *the* Mongoose's troublemaking list was a hoverbike depot located a block from her old elementary school. Once it was a Little League baseball diamond, and home to both the Cold Spring Junior Yankees and the Hudson Valley Little Pirates. Parents cheered from the stands while Mr. Consuela sold Italian ices from his cart. Now the kids, the cart, and the parents were gone and the field was a parking lot for alien motorcycles. There were twelve bikes parked there that night, and thanks to Julep, ten of them were already toast. She scampered toward number eleven.

The hoverbikes boggled her mind. Though she'd

watched them whip down her road for the last six months, she still didn't know how they worked, but she had discovered their major design flaw—the engines were easy to sabotage. If you poured a cup of sugar into the fuel tank, the motor exploded. She slipped off her backpack, reached inside, and snatched the bag of sugar she'd brought from home; then, with nimble fingers, she unscrewed the bike's fuel cap, only to face a belly-emptying stink that invaded her nose and traveled all the way to her lungs. Whatever the alien bugs used as fuel was foul. It smelled like a dirty diaper forgotten at a hot campground.

Tilting the bag, she emptied the remaining sugar into the tank and watched the chemical reaction. The fuel fizzed and popped and threatened to spill out onto the ground. Quickly, she twisted the cap back on and tossed the empty sack onto the ground. She wasn't normally a litterbug, but she wanted the invaders to know what had happened to their machines. More importantly, she wanted the town to know. Folks were afraid to fight back against the occupation. Her neighbors thought they needed laser cannons or a thermo blaster to fight the Plague, but all the destructive stuff they could ever hope for was in their own kitchen cabinets.

"All right, *the* Mongoose. You've done enough. It's time to go," Truman said.

"Almost, big brother," Julep said.

"Almost?"

She dashed across the field to the last of the hover-bikes. She had purposely left this one alone. She had plans for it. Settling onto its seat, she clenched the handles and eyed the control panel between her legs. It was a big, bulky vehicle, designed for a much larger bug body, but she was sure she could drive it. She scanned the controls for the power button and pressed it, and the bike came to life with a low hum. The entire machine rose a couple of feet off the ground. The engine's vibrations ran through her entire body. Such power!

"Don't even think about it," her brother snapped. "You can't steal a hoverbike."

"But I can, big brother. In fact, I'm already doing it." Julep studied the field for bug soldiers, and seeing it was clear, she gave the handlebars a twist and blasted forward, cutting through the tall outfield grass. The surge was more than she expected. She nearly slid off the back of the bike.

"What is wrong with your brain?" her brother cried.

"Nothing! I'm perfectly sane. Stealing a hoverbike will grow the rebellion!" she shouted over the wind.

"What rebellion? It's just us!"

"Exactly. We need to do something daring if we're going to inspire new recruits."

"There's a fence!" Truman cried just as the front end of the bike slammed through the high chain-link fence

4

encircling the field, leaving a ragged opening behind it. "Subtle."

"Relax. I totally got away with it," she told him, just as a video screen on the control panel came to life. In the center was a green dot, which she assumed was her. Behind the dot were eleven more dots, and they were chasing her. "Uh-oh."

"Uh-oh? What's uh-oh?" Truman asked.

"It's nothing," she said just as a blast of blue energy flew past her and exploded in the road. Gravel and pebbles showered down on her head. "Just a few bugs chasing me."

"You said the sugar would wreck their engines!"

"It will. It just takes a little while, I guess," she muttered.

"How much longer?" he asked.

Probably longer than she had. She searched the bike's controls for something that might keep her from ending up a stain on the road. There were so many buttons, all of them glowing and demanding her attention, and all of them in the strange Plague language she couldn't read. "Shields . . . Shields . . . Where are the shields? Maybe this one?"

She pressed the button and watched a faint white light encase the bike and herself.

"Look at that! First try!" she cheered, just as another energy blast crashed nearby. Luckily, the shields absorbed most of the impact, but she still had to wrestle with the bike to keep it under control.

One of the bugs pulled alongside her on the left, another on the right. They screeched and hissed at her while waving their sonic blasters.

"Pull over or be destroyed!" one of them shrieked.

Julep twisted the accelerator even more and barreled ahead in a shocking burst of speed. The bugs vanished behind her in a cloud of dust. There was no way she was pulling over. She couldn't get caught. The bugs would figure out who she was and arrest everyone she loved. They'd drag them to the mother ship. A kid from school had been taken there six months ago, and he hadn't come back.

"This is your last warning, human!" a bug said as it matched her speed. "Stop the bike and surrender or you will be—"

Suddenly, the bug's hoverbike exploded. The driver was thrown off, and he tumbled down the rocky cliff bordering the road. A moment later, she heard another bike behind her crash. One by one, all the bikes were engulfed in flames in her rearview mirrors.

"Never underestimate the destructive nature of sugar!" she cried.

"Yes, you get a gold star for today," Truman said. "Now ditch the bike and come home."

He was barely finished with his sentence when something huge and black fell from the sky.

"Fudge!" she gasped.

"It's a Dragonfly! Get out of there!" Truman cried.

Dragonflies were compact attack ships about the size of a minivan, designed to destroy tanks and fighter jets. Through the red sheen of its cockpit glass, Julep saw the Plague pilot staring back at her. She was pretty sure bugs couldn't smile, but this one seemed pleased, especially when two panels on the front slid aside, revealing a dozen plasma cannons. There was no way her hoverbike's shields were strong enough to take a direct hit, let alone twelve of them. Retreat was her only option, so with a twist of the accelerator, Julep sped away, just missing a cannon blast that ripped apart the ground.

"Don't say it. I know you want to say it."

"Don't say what?" her brother asked. "You mean don't say that I told you not to steal the bike?"

The Dragonfly fired again. The blast missed her, but the shock wave nearly knocked her off the bike.

"All right, big brother. Get me out of here," she said

"Head toward Breakneck Ridge on 9D. It's your only chance."

Route 9D was the highway out of town, a curvy and narrow two-lane road that burrowed through the side of a mountain. Her brother didn't have to explain his plan. It was brilliant, if she could make it there alive. She pushed the bike to its top speed and accelerated into the turns in hopes of putting some space between herself and the ship. It didn't help. The Dragonfly was fast and agile. It was practically glued to her.

"Make a left at Stone Avenue!"

She slid across the intersection, sideswiped a parked car, and then righted herself. Without the shields she would have totaled the bike and probably broken a leg.

"They're firing!" her brother warned.

An explosion lifted her into the air. She lost control and steered into someone's yard, hopping over a kiddie pool and crashing through a wooden fence. It was chaos. In the days before the Plague's invasion, these yards would have been full of people enjoying the night air. But now those same people were huddled in their homes, too terrified to break the Plague's curfew.

"It's coming around the other side. They're trying to cut you off," her brother warned. "Head east!"

At the end of the street, Julep leaned into another turn and pointed the bike toward the fir-covered hills and Route 9D. Bear Mountain was to her right and the Hudson River flowed alongside her to the left. The roar of the Dragonfly's engines hung overhead. The craft flew through power lines, snapping them in two and sending the broken ends to the road below. They twisted on the asphalt like angry rattlesnakes.

"They're trying to crush you," Truman warned.

He was right. The Dragonfly's belly was only a few feet above her now. *How ironic,* she thought. *I'm about to get squished by a bug.*

Another twist of the accelerator and she zipped ahead before the ship could smash her, but she wasn't out of danger yet. Explosions rocked the ground, pulverizing pavement and sending gravel and dust everywhere. A blast hit so close she lost control and the hoverbike tipped. She skidded along the concrete, tumbling and rolling out of control.

"Get up, Julep! You have to get up!" Truman cried.

She scampered to her feet and struggled to get the huge bike upright, but it was too heavy. She couldn't lift it.

"Leave it!" her brother shouted in her ear.

She had no choice. Still shaken from the fall, she tried to run, but her legs and brain weren't on speaking terms. Her ears were ringing. Her head was pounding. The best she could do was hobble forward, unsure of her direction in the dust and debris.

"It's right there," her brother promised. "Just keep going. I don't think they see it."

"I don't see it, either!" she said to him.

And then the air cleared, and the road became a tunnel. Once inside, Julep turned just in time to watch the Dragonfly crash into the mountain's rocky face. A sonic boom sent her flailing onto her back. Fire rose three stories, and thick black smoke swallowed everything. Dazed, she got to her knees and watched the broken ship crash to the ground in pieces, right on top of her hoverbike.

"Julep? Julep! Are you okay?" her brother cried. "Talk to me! Tell me you're all right!"

She pulled off her mask, freeing her long black hair, then pushed her glasses up the bridge of her nose and frowned.

"I'm fine," she replied. "But I'm gonna need a ride home."

ome. Finn could barely believe he was back. Having spent what felt like weeks bouncing through time, running from bounty hunters, Time Rangers, and a monster bent on destroying reality itself, he had wondered if he would ever see it again. He stood back and did his best to absorb it all—the cool breeze, the smell of the trees, the lightning bugs burning trails through the air. Not long ago he had detested everything about this house, the town, and everyone in it. Now he couldn't be any happier to find himself in the backyard.

"Be kind to yourself, kid, and when you see your dad, tell him ol' Zeke says hello," the strange, time-traveling cowboy said to him. Zeke had arrived as an enemy and was leaving as a friend, having given Finn the final clue to finding his long-lost father, Asher Foley. Finn wished Zeke would come along to help bring him home, but the alien had his copper-colored hand on his time-traveling lasso. He was eager to go.

"I will," Finn promised.

"Oh, and, son, be careful," Zeke said. He twirled the rope and it burned hot with flames until finally slicing a hole in space. "This world ain't the one you left."

"What do you mean?" Finn asked, but Zeke didn't answer. He waved and stepped through the portal, leaving a ring of smoke in his place.

"How did you escape?"

Finn turned to find his mom and his little sister, Kate, charging across the lawn. They were both in a panic.

"Escape what?"

"Get inside!" Mom cried, and together they dragged him into the house. When the door was locked, they went from room to room, flipping off lights, shutting windows, and drawing the curtains. Soon the trio was standing in the dark. Before Finn could ask what was happening, Kate hurried over to the front window and peered out at the street.

"There's twenty of them out there, but I don't think they saw him," she said.

"Twenty who?" Finn asked. Kate was always a little weird, but Mom was acting super strange, too. When they didn't answer, he walked over to look for himself. Mom yanked him back before he got a chance.

"Are you crazy? They'll come in here and take you away again. Oh, Finn, we've missed you so much. Did they hurt you?"

"Mom, I don't know what you're talking about," he said, squirming out of her grip. He pulled the drapes aside to see what was causing them so much anxiety. What was outside made him wish he hadn't. Dozens of heavily armed, man-sized locusts were marching down his street.

"The bugs are back? When did that happen?" The shock knocked the wind out of him. He bent over, feeling like everything was spinning. It wasn't possible. He thought he'd sent them so far away they'd never find Earth again.

"What have they done to you?" Mom said. "Finn, the Plague never went away. They've been here since they conquered the planet."

He gaped outside a second time, just to make sure his eyes weren't fooling him. The neighborhood was a mess. Cars were deserted in the middle of the street, a broken fire hydrant emptied water into the gutters, and a crashed helicopter was sticking out of the roof of a house across the street.

"But we fought them back," he argued, until the

truth set him straight. Maybe he hadn't sent the bugs packing. Maybe everything he knew, everything he had done to save the world, had never happened. Now he understood Zeke's warning. This wasn't the world he left before he went back in time.

"Zeke!" he shouted, hoping the Time Ranger was watching him from his ranch. He would know what to do. Zeke could go back and fix whatever he had messed up. "You have to come back. Everything is wrong!"

"He's sick, Mom," Kate said. "They did something to him on the mother ship. No one ever comes back from there the same way."

Mom pressed her hand against his forehead to check for a fever.

"He's just confused. Maybe if we show him what's under the floorboards, it will help his memories," Mom said.

Together, they hurried him upstairs to his old bedroom. Mom and Kate pushed his bed aside, then got on their hands and knees to pull up some loose floorboards. Once those were set aside, Mom reached into the hole in the floor and came back out with a burlap sack. She shoved it into Finn's hands.

"What is this?"

"Open it," Kate said.

He tore the bag open and found a large egg-shaped

object inside. When he flipped it over, he realized it was a robotic head with a glass screen for a face—a face he knew very well.

"Highbeam!" he exclaimed, even though this too was not possible. Highbeam had returned to his home planet on the other side of the universe with his partner, Dax, his ex-wife, and his twenty-five children . . . but here he was. At least, here was his head. That couldn't be a good sign. Thank goodness the glass lit up and a series of alien icons streamed across his face, ultimately forming an exclamation point.

"Little man!"

"Where's the rest of your body, buddy?" Finn asked.

The icons morphed into an arrow pointing toward the sky.

"The bugs have it. Hey! How did you escape?"

"He doesn't remember," Kate said. "Do you think they did something to his brain?"

"Please tell your sister I'm not talking to her," Highbeam said.

"Are we doing this again?" Kate cried.

"Highbeam is upset that we have to hide him," Mom explained.

"Tell your mother that I am not talking to her, either, but if I were, I would ask her how she would feel if someone shoved her into a bag and stuffed her under the floorboards."

"The Plague searches our house once a week, High-beam," Mom said. "You know that. It's the only way to make sure they don't find you."

Highbeam let out a dismissive harrumph.

"Listen, it's great to see everyone, really, but I have to tell you something and it's going to be hard to believe," Finn said, interrupting the spat. "Though it shouldn't, when you think about everything we've gone through. It's a long story and I'll do the best I can to explain, but this isn't supposed to be happening."

"This?" Kate asked.

"Yeah, this. Everything," he said, waving his hands. "The bugs didn't conquer Earth. They aren't in the streets right now. I was never in a prison on the mother ship."

"Is it possible he has space cooties or something?" Kate asked Highbeam.

"It's possible," Highbeam replied. "I'm sorry, kid, but facts are facts: the bugs are in charge. Listen, I'm happy to see you, but you should never have come back here. The whole armada will be looking for you. This is the first place they'll come."

Someone pounded on the door downstairs. It was so loud it shook Finn's bedroom windows. It sounded like the door might fly off its hinges. Mom's eyes grew to twice their usual size.

"That's them," Mom whispered.

"I am Sergeant Mix Toro, of the Plague High Guard," a voice boomed from the front yard. *"Open your home and prepare for a search, pinkskins! Cooperation is in your best interest."*

"Don't panic. They may not know you're here. It could be just another search," Mom said. "Finn, take Highbeam and hide in the secret room."

"What secret room?"

"You have until the count of five. At that time we will vaporize the door and drag you out!" Toro threatened. Instead of counting, the soldiers outside rubbed their back legs together, making loud clicks. As always, the sound crushed Finn's ears.

"You're not going down there," Finn said to his family.

"We have to answer the door," Mom said. "Now go. Hide!"

She and Kate went downstairs, but Finn didn't do as his mom had told him. From the hall, he watched her open the door. Four huge Plague soldiers barged into the house and pushed them aside. The bugs studied them with their huge black eyes.

"Where is he?" Toro demanded. His exoskeleton was pale green, and he had orange markings on his face. He was wearing a jacket covered with copper medals and was carrying a shock blaster.

"Who?" Mom asked, playing dumb.

"Don't treat us like fools, human! We know Finn Foley is here," the leader growled.

"My son is a prisoner on the mother ship. You should check there first before you come here."

"Watch your tone." He raised a claw to hit her, but Kate stepped in the way.

"Finn isn't here!" Kate shouted.

Toro snatched her by the back of her shirt and lifted her off the floor. Kate kicked and swung her arms, clearly hoping to hit the much bigger bug, but he was just out of her reach.

"Keep your hopper quiet, woman, or I will silence her myself," the soldier threatened Mom. "Search every inch of this house!"

His soldiers went to work turning everything upside down. Closets were opened, their contents scattered. A soldier in the kitchen smashed plates and glasses as it searched the cabinets. Finn heard something spill onto the floor.

"How would my brother hide inside a box of cereal?" Kate cried.

"Shut up!" a bug roared.

Finn was about to rush down the stairs when Highbeam stopped him.

"You'll get them killed, kid. Do what your mother told you. Hide."

Finn didn't like it, but he knew the robot was right. He crept into his mother's room and quietly shut the door. Once inside, he immediately noticed that something was different. The walk-in closet was missing. In fact, there was a wall where a wall had never been before.

"There's a latch by the window," Highbeam whispered.

Finn searched for it while a soldier's heavy feet stomped up the stairs. When he found it, the fake wall rolled aside, revealing the missing walk-in closet. He hurried inside, secured the wall back into place, and sat with Highbeam in the dark.

"We know you're here, boy," a voice hissed. "You can't hide from us."

The word *shhhhh* scrolled across Highbeam's face. Finn clapped his hand across his mouth and nose, in case the sound of his breathing alerted the monster to his hiding place.

The soldier tore his mom's room apart. Through the wall Finn heard glass shattering and furniture tipping onto the floor. It sounded as if her bed was flipped over. Soon enough, the bug got bored with wrecking things and stomped back downstairs.

"How did the bugs get your body?" Finn whispered to Highbeam.

"How could you forget that, kid? We were on the mother ship trying to dismantle the engines when Kraven cornered us and— Wow. You are sick, aren't you?"

Finn shook his head. "They're trashing the place. Does this kind of thing happen to Mom and Kate a lot?"

"Unfortunately, yes. The bugs show up about once a week and tear everything apart," Highbeam replied. "They're still trying to figure out who has the magic lunchbox, and unfortunately, your mom and Kate are their top suspects."

"The lunchbox? Dude, the lunchbox was destroyed, along with that funky machine on my . . ."

Finn's words trailed away as he lifted his shirt. There, much to his bewilderment, was a familiar alien technology fused to his chest. The lights inside it blinked and buzzed as if to say "Hello, again."

"The wormhole generator is back!" Finn cried. "I can't believe it."

"Did you hear something?" one of the bugs shouted to his partner. He sounded as if he was in the hall.

"I think it came from the little girl's room!"

"Kid, you have to keep it down," Highbeam whispered.

"I'm sorry. I just didn't expect to ever see this gizmo again. Is the lunchbox here?"

Highbeam's face grew bright, illuminating the dark

closet. There were old clothes on racks and a collection of cardboard boxes stacked against the wall.

"Safe and sound in one of those boxes," Highbeam said.

Hidden beneath a duffel bag was a cardboard box with *Asher* written on it. Finn knew it well. The box was full of his dad's things, left behind when he disappeared. Finn tore it open and dug through a stack of college sweatshirts and concert T-shirts. He came across a lasso and a cowboy hat. He couldn't help but smile. His dad had never seemed like the kind of guy to wear something so big and bold, but then again, Asher didn't seem like the kind of guy who would travel through time capturing criminals, either. Finn didn't have a clue how the lasso worked, but he'd seen Zeke use one and knew it was powerful. Maybe this one would come in handy when he found his dad.

At the bottom of the box, Finn spotted a pink plastic handle. The moment his fingers touched it, a loud rumbling shook the floor. It worked!

Finn gasped. "I can't believe it!" He pulled it out. It was the bright pink rainbow-covered sparkly unicorn lunchbox that allowed him to go anywhere in the universe.

"That thing is making a racket," Highbeam said.

The robot was right. Finn dropped it on the floor and the noise stopped.

"This is a huge stroke of luck for us, big guy," he said. "We can use this to find my dad, I hope. But first we need to find Pre'at," Finn said. "Where is she?"

"You don't . . . Sorry, kid. This hole in your memory is going to take some getting used to. She's on the mother ship," Highbeam said. "She got arrested with us when we tried to stop the invasion. I suspect the bugs are forcing her to use her big brain to invent weapons for them."

"Then we have to rescue her, 'cause I need her big brain, too," Finn said. "Are you ready to get your body back?"

"You know it!"

"Good, but let's take care of the bug infestation downstairs first," he said, scooping up his friend's head with one hand and the lunchbox with the other. The closet rumbled and the device on his chest crackled with life. He shut his eyes, focused on the universe, and watched it all unfold in his mind—gas giants, dual nebulas, mysterious worlds, asteroid belts, alien life-forms. The lunchbox showed him billions and billions of places to go, but the cosmos could wait. He had some-place much closer in mind. As the lunchbox bounced in his hand, he watched the lid slowly unzip itself. Wild bolts of white-hot electricity shot out and a shimmer-ing portal appeared—no larger than a quarter at first, but it grew and grew. Inside it, planets and asteroids revealed themselves, then meteors and comets, all spiraling in a beautiful whirlpool of stars. When the opening was large enough, Finn jumped in, and in a flash he and Highbeam disappeared. A second later, he popped up in his sister's room, where a bug soldier was hefting her bed aside. Finn tapped him on the shoulder to get his attention.

"Looking for me?" the boy asked as he looped his arm around the bug and opened another portal. When it materialized, he dragged the startled soldier inside it and they came out in his bedroom, where they found a second bug emptying his closet.

"Dude! That's my stuff."

He shoved the two bugs into a new portal, and they all came out in the living room, where they found the last two Plague soldiers threatening his mother.

"Mom, I think someone left the door open. The place is full of insects," Finn said as he tossed her Highbeam's head. Before the bugs could react, he opened a final wormhole and pushed all the surprised invaders into it. This time, however, Finn didn't go along for the ride.

"Where did you send them?" Highbeam asked as he watched the whirlpool shrink into nothing.

"The moon," Finn replied.

"They'll send more," Kate warned. "They'll drag you back to the mother ship."

"They won't have to," Finn said. "Highbeam and I are headed there now."

"What? Finn! No!" his mom cried.

"Mom, I have to. Dad is counting on me," Finn said.

"Dad?" Kate cried. "What does he have to do with this?"

"Everything," Finn said. "I know, I know, I'm still not making sense, but there's too much to explain and no time to do it. Just know that I found him. He didn't leave us. He was taken, and I'm going to bring him home."

"My brother definitely has space cooties," Kate said.

3

Finn changed into some clean clothes and dug his backpack out of his closet. Mom, Kate, and High-beam circled him, tossing a million questions in his direction, but there was no time to explain such a complicated story. After scarfing down a couple of peanut butter and jelly sandwiches and giving himself a much-needed tooth-brushing, he packed his father's lasso, the unicorn lunchbox, and Highbeam's head into his backpack, then kissed his mom and his sister goodbye.

"I'll be back as soon as I can," he promised, "and I'll bring Dad with me. He'll fix all of this. He can put the world back the way it's supposed to be."

Finn darted outside, doing his best to stay in the shadows. It was easier than it should have been. All the streetlights were either busted or burned out, and there wasn't a soul in sight. Now that he was outside, he got a look at Cold Spring. It was a disaster. Across the street he saw the remains of Ms. Pressman's house. A fire had gutted it, taking the neighboring houses as well. All down Elm Street, garbage was piled high in front of every house, and litter blew through like a filthy tornado. Cars sat abandoned with their doors flung open, as if the owners had screeched to a stop and fled. Broken bicycles, scooters, and skateboards lay everywhere. A motorcycle lay on its side, the tires deflated. The smell of smoke was everywhere. It burned his eyes and nostrils. The whole scene was unsettling, as if he had stepped into a scary movie and there was no way out.

The only noise came from above. Hovering overhead was the Plague mother ship, so enormous it blocked out the moon and stars. A gigantic white tube snaked from its belly and impaled the ground not far away. Finn understood the tube's terrible function: this was why the bugs took over his world. The tube was slowly consuming Earth's resources. When it was finished, the planet would be a dusty husk and the bugs would move on.

"We stopped this once, Highbeam," Finn said.

"As you keep saying. If you want to tell me how we did it, I'd be happy to try it again," Highbeam called from inside the backpack.

"I don't know if we can. We had friends—Dax was here, and my school principal, Mr. Doogan, and Deputies Dortch and Day, plus a dozen aliens on the council, and your kids," Finn explained.

"My kids were here? How? Let me guess. It's a long story, right? Well, I hope you're right about your dad. I don't know how one man is going to fight off the armada."

"Have faith, big guy," Finn said.

"I'm trying." the robot said. "I just don't understand why we're creeping around in the bushes."

"'Cause there are two more people we need if we want to succeed—Lincoln and Julep," Finn explained.

"Who?"

"They're my best friends. I know you don't remember, but we couldn't have saved the world without them."

"Kid, I don't forget things. If it happened, it's stored in my memory cards," Highbeam said. "I have never met anyone named Lincoln or Julep."

The robot was right. He had never met Lincoln and Julep because Finn changed the past. Looking around, he wondered if he had made the right decision. At the time, giving his friend Lincoln the greatest gift of all— his mother—had seemed like the kindest thing to do. Mrs. Sidana died in a car accident when Lincoln was a little boy, but the time machine allowed him to save her. Finn knew there might be unpredictable consequences, but how could he let Lincoln's mom die if he could prevent it? How could he ever look his best friend in the eye again, knowing he could have saved his mom and didn't do it?

Finn ducked around the corner of Washington Street, where a crushed tank blocked the road. A fighter plane was upside down on top of someone's garage, and there was a massive crater where several houses had once stood. He caught a glimpse of someone watching from a nearby house, but they drew the curtains and shut off the lights.

"Hasn't anyone tried to fight back?" he asked Highbeam.

"Don't be too harsh, little man. Earthlings thought aliens were only in movies and TV shows until about six months ago. The military and the police did their best, but they were no match for bug technology. People lost hope. I can't blame them. I come from a planet that was conquered by the Plague, too," Highbeam said, reminding Finn of his home world of Nemeth.

"You never lost hope. You joined a rebellion," Finn said.

"We also had access to spaceships and laser guns. Humans are a quite a bit more primitive."

"I can't believe no one is organizing a resistance."

"I've heard about small groups plotting and planning attacks, but most get crushed before they can even get started. Honestly, the most successful of them is a kid running around town calling herself the Mongoose. She's caused a lot of havoc for the bugs, but she's just one person."

Finn hurried down Whitehead Street, past several burned-out police cars, until he got to a little house in the middle of the block. The lawn was dry, as were a few crumbling potted flowers. The place could have used a coat of paint, too. A steel ramp led from the front door to the driveway, where a large black van was parked. When Finn got close to it, he heard its engine ticking as it cooled in the night air. Someone must have just been driving it.

"Why did we stop?" Highbeam asked from inside the backpack.

"We're at Julep's house," Finn said. He reached into his pants pocket and took out a phone. It had once belonged to Julep, his Julep. It was the only thing he had left from his time-traveling adventure. He turned it on and went through a quick search of the photos stored inside it. Yes! This was the proof he would need if this Julep didn't remember him.

He took a deep breath, called on all his courage, and rang the doorbell. The chime seemed like a foghorn in the quiet neighborhood.

The door opened an inch and an eye peered through the crack.

"It's past curfew! Go away before you cause us all trouble!"

Finn recognized the voice. It belonged to Mrs. Li, Julep's mother. Her accent was a quirky combination of Japanese and Appalachian. She and her husband had immigrated to the United States and raised Julep in Silva, North Carolina, before moving to upstate New York. Finn adored Julep's family. Mrs. Li's refrigerator held an endless supply of kyoho-ade—a fruity drink made from kyoho grapes. Finn could drink gallons of it. Unfortunately, Mrs. Li's friendly personality was gone. It was clear he was not welcome and there would be no kyoho-ade today.

"My name is Finn Foley. I go to school with Julep. I really need to speak to her," he said.

"There hasn't been any school for six months," she replied.

"I've been away for a while. It's very important."

Mrs. Li eyed him with suspicion, then opened the door just wide enough to drag him inside. He watched her go to work locking a dozen dead bolts and chains while Julep's father stood on the other side of the room wielding a baseball bat.

"Why did you come to our house this late at night?" he demanded. "The bugs could have followed you."

"He says he knows Julep from school," Mrs. Li cried. "Julep! There is a strange boy here for you."

A moment later, Julep Li stepped into the room. Finn's belly did a flip-flop. The girl always sparked the same reaction, a combination of barfy and happy, but this time it was turned all the way to a hundred. The last time he'd seen Julep she was sick, fighting off the power of a monster determined to steal her body. Finn hadn't been positive she had escaped, but here she was, healthy and wearing the same big smile that made him dizzy. The only thing different was the bag of frozen peas she pressed against her elbow.

"Julep, do you know this boy?" Mr. Li asked. He looked like he was hoping the answer would be no so he could use his bat.

"Finn Foley?"

"Is he part of this thing you and your brother do?" her mother asked.

"I don't know what you're talking about," Julep said.

"Your parents are not dumb. You two are up to something," Mr. Li said. "We see the mud on your shoes, and tonight Truman tore out of here in the van. He brought you back covered in bruises."

"I fell off my bike," she said.

"You don't have a bike. Whatever it is you're doing it had better stop," Mrs. Li said, then turned to Finn. "And you'd better not be getting my daughter into trouble."

"Leave him alone, Ma," Julep said as she snatched Finn by the hand. "We're going to Truman's room. Finn wants to see his drone. Right, Finn?"

"Um, right," Finn lied.

Truman's bedroom was designed to accommodate his wheelchair, and looked more like the headquarters in a spy novel than a place to sleep. There were three desks, each overflowing with an array of electronics. There were drones, walkie-talkies, police scanners, and a laptop showing a map of Cold Spring. Mr. and Mrs. Li were right: their kids were up to something. The moment Julep shut the door, she and her brother peppered him with questions.

"How did you escape?" she asked.

"Are they chasing you?" Truman pressed.

"Did they torture you?"

"What was it like on the ship?"

"Could you make a map of it?"

"How many bugs are up there?"

"What did they feed you?"

"Were there other humans in the jails?"

"Wait!" Finn interrupted. The interrogation was giving him a headache, and he had questions of his own. "You two know me?"

"Of course. You're a legend," Julep said. "Finn Foley, the boy who took on the bugs, and you're in our house!"

"Would it be weird to ask for an autograph?" Truman said.

Finn's heart sank. Julep and her brother knew him from rumors, but it was obvious she didn't have any memory of their friendship. He'd known it was a long shot, another consequence of fooling around with the past, but he had hoped that their bond defied space and time.

"Wait!" Julep cried. "You came to join the revolution!"

"No way!" Truman said. "This is huge."

"I don't know what you're talking about," Finn said.

"It's cool. No one can hear us in here," Truman said, giving him a wink. "I've got an audio scrambler on my room so the bugs can't listen in."

"How did you figure out my secret identity?" she asked.

Finn shook his head. The siblings were talking so fast he was having trouble keeping up.

"I'm the Mongoose," she said.

Truman proudly gestured to his drones.

"Oh, yeah, I heard about you. Listen, I didn't come to join your fight. I came here for your help. You see . . . Listen, the story is complicated. I tried to tell my family, but they didn't understand, and you're not going to believe me, either, so I'm just going to skip ahead to the proof," he said. He placed her phone into her hands.

"Hey! How did you get my phone?" she asked, then reached into her pocket and pulled out an identical copy. "Wait. This is weird. How do you have a phone that's exactly like mine? There's even a scratch on the back."

"You gave it to me," he said. "In the future."

He braced for their laughter, but it didn't come.

"No way," Julep whispered.

"If there's anyone in the world who will believe me, it's you, Julep. All the books you carry around about time travel and aliens and Bigfoots . . . well, a lot of it is real, and I know you don't remember, but you experienced it yourself—except for the Bigfoots, but apparently they're out there in the woods waiting to be discovered."

"I think the bugs did something to your brain," Truman said.

"Hush," Julep said to her brother. She opened up the picture app on her phone and scrolled through photos. With each one, her eyes got bigger and bigger behind her glasses. She showed one to her brother, but he rolled his eyes.

"They're obviously fake," Truman said.

Finn frowned at Truman's disbelief, but he wasn't

beaten yet. He took off his backpack, unzipped it, and removed Highbeam's head.

"I thought you might say that," Finn replied.

"About time," the robot grumbled. "It smells like socks and baloney in there!"

"No way!" Truman cried, rolling forward to snatch the robot's head from Finn. He turned it over and over, spinning it around in his hands to examine every side.

"Hey, buster! You're going to make me barf," the robot cried.

"This is Highbeam. He's a Class One Demo-Bot from the planet Nemeth," Finn said. "He's your friend, too."

"So *he* says." Highbeam's face lit up with icons. They formed a cuckoo clock. "Did he give you guys the 'we saved the world in an alternate past' talk yet? Honestly, I think the bugs dropped him on his head."

"Why are you showing us this, Finn Foley?" Julep asked.

"Like I said, I need your help, Julep. I have something important to do, something that can fix the whole world, but I don't think I can do it without you. Every time things have turned upside down, you were by my side to put them back. You're kind of my good-luck charm."

Julep's cheeks flashed pink for a second, but only Finn noticed.

"What's this thing you need to do?"

Finn explained the best he could—about his dad, Pre'at, and the mother ship.

"I'm in," she said without hesitation. "Gimme a second."

"Julep, no!" Truman cried.

"Big brother, we've been talking about the mother ship for six months," Julep said. "You're going to have to come up with a story to tell Mom and Dad so they won't worry."

Julep darted out of Truman's room.

"This is not cool!" her brother shouted.

"Wow! I can't believe I met *the* Mongoose," Highbeam said during the awkward silence. "How cool is it that she's your sister? You two remind me of my days with my partner Dax Dargon. We're pretty famous trouble-makers on my world, if I do say so myself."

Julep returned seconds later. Her backpack was strapped to her shoulders and stuffed so full it was a wonder she could zip it closed.

"Julep, you can't do this," Truman said.

"We might never get another chance," she said as she patted her backpack and winked.

Something unsaid passed between the siblings, but Finn didn't press them to explain.

"All right, Finn Foley. Let's get into some trouble."

Finn reached into his pack for the unicorn lunchbox. The rumble caused some of Truman's electronics to skitter off his desk.

"That's . . . different," Julep said. "Do you think this is the best time to have a snack?"

"This is how we're getting to the mother ship, but first we have to make another stop." Finn closed his eyes tight and focused on his next destination. The room shook, the lunchbox bounced, and electricity supercharged the air. A second later, a spinning whirlpool opened in the middle of Truman's bedroom.

"Finn Foley, you're the coolest kid I've ever met," Julep said.

It was Finn's turn to blush. He scooped up Highbeam's head and took Julep by the hand.

"Don't do anything dumb," Truman called.

Julep laughed. "Then why go at all?"

Finn cried, "Hang on!" and together they leaped into the portal.

4

The duo was spit out inside a cluttered pool house full of inflatable rafts and bottles of chlorine. Their sudden arrival caused a calamity, and things fell off shelves and spilled onto the floor in heaving glugs.

"O! M! G!" Julep cried. "We were . . . and now we're . . . This is crazy! How?"

"It's complicated," Finn said. "Do you believe me now?"

"I'm all in, Finn Foley." Julep was so excited she didn't mind shaking pool cleaner out of her shoe. "Though the landings are a little rough."

"I didn't want anyone to see us," he replied as he slipped off his pack. In went the lunchbox, and out came Highbeam.

"What is this mess?" the robot asked.

"We're in Lincoln's pool house."

"Another one of your best friends no one remembers?" the robot asked.

"The sarcasm is getting a little thick," Finn said, and turned to Julep. "Don't mind him. He's grumpy without his body. Lincoln is the boy you saw in the pictures. The three of us are . . . or were inseparable."

"Before the time travel," Julep said. Finn was grateful that she was catching on quickly. "What do you think the odds are he'll remember you any better than I do?"

Finn shrugged. Was it possible Lincoln knew him? That somehow they had met and become friends? Sure, but it wasn't likely.

He slowly opened the pool house door and peeked outside. The glow from the pool's underwater lights bathed Lincoln's house in a faint green glow. It was a big, fancy place, probably the nicest home in all of Cold Spring. Lincoln's father was a very successful surgeon. When Finn had met him, Lincoln and his father had been drifting apart, but when the Plague showed up, they had worked together to help destroy the mother ship's engines. Finn wondered what the two of them were like now that Mrs. Sidana was alive and well.

Along with Julep and Highbeam, he crept quietly toward a bay window where the orange flicker of a fireplace danced on the glass. He heard the distant tinkling of piano keys, and someone was singing. The window didn't give him many clues, so he hurried the trio around the corner of the house to find a better view. Finally, they caught sight of Dr. Sidana sitting on a couch. A woman was playing a grand piano nearby. Finn guessed she was Lincoln's mother, but he couldn't pay attention to her. His eyes were glued to the third person in the room. Between the adults was Lincoln Sidana, and one look at him told Finn that his friend's life had taken a very different path than before. Gone were his sloppy pants and shirts, replaced by a forest-green blazer adorned with a golden school crest sewn onto the lapel, a white dress shirt, and pressed khakis. His shaggy, unkempt hair was now neat and trim. Oddest of all was the dancing. Lincoln was spinning around his living room in a complex choreography of kicks and turns, all while belting out a song at the top of his lungs. Lincoln had a naturally beautiful voice, something Finn had discovered not long ago, but this Lincoln clearly took lessons. Every high note was pitch perfect, and came with a wink or a pointed finger in the air like he was firing off imaginary pistols.

"O-klahoma, where the wind comes sweeping down the plain," Lincoln sang.

"This is the kid you want to take on a rescue mission to an alien spaceship?" Highbeam asked.

"No," Finn said. "I mean, he wasn't all glee-club

before. My Lincoln was the biggest bully this town has ever seen."

Finn watched in dumbfounded amazement. Lincoln knew the whole song, the choreography, and how to move around the room to make the biggest impression on his two-person audience. When the song came to an end, he took a bow to thunderous applause from his mom and dad.

"That was splendid, Lincoln," Finn heard the boy's mother say.

"Your hard work has really paid off, son," his father added.

"Well, as long as it looks good on my college applications," Lincoln said.

"Lincoln, you're only eleven. College is . . . well, it's a long way off," Dr. Sidana said.

"It's never too soon to plan for the future," Lincoln said matter-of-factly.

"College?" Julep said. "That's some serious wishful thinking. The planet is being eaten by gigantic locusts. By the time he's ready for college, Earth is going to be a dried-out desert."

Julep was right. His best friend was learning choreography for a future he might never see. It was delusional, but more than that, it was downright strange. Finn's Lincoln never once mentioned his plans for the future. He was only eleven, after all, and, well, Lincoln didn't seem the type to think that far ahead. He could barely commit to what he planned to eat for lunch, let alone what he was going to do in seven years. All of it caused Finn's heart to sink into his gut. There was no point in wishful thinking anymore. Changing the past had turned his funny, messy, grumpy friend into an overachieving actor with jazz hands and high kicks.

"Are you sure we need him?" Julep asked.

"He's been by our side every time," Finn said, pushing his doubts deep into his belly. "C'mon, let's talk to him."

They scurried to Lincoln's bedroom window and waited. His room wasn't the upturned disaster Finn remembered. Everything was tidy and in its place. His clothes were folded and put away. Even the shirts were on hangers. Finn was pretty sure his Lincoln didn't even own a hanger. Eventually, Lincoln entered. He took off his blazer and laid it on an ironing board, then used an electric steamer to remove some wrinkles. When he was satisfied, he put it back on and stepped in front of the mirror to admire his work. Finally, he sat down at his desk, turned on a lamp, and began to read from a pile of textbooks.

"He's studying," Julep said in surprise. "There's no school."

"Kid, either grab him or go," Highbeam grumbled as

the icons on his face turned into a frown. "I'm sick of hanging out in your backpack."

"Just let me think this through. I don't want to scare him off. We're total strangers to him, and—"

Julep banged on Lincoln's window.

"What are you doing?" Finn cried.

"Speeding things up," Julep said.

"Thank you," Highbeam said.

Lincoln peered out at them, then tentatively opened his window.

"Go away," he said. "We have no room for beggars."

"We're not beggars," Julep cried.

"My name is Finn—"

"Foley," Lincoln interrupted. "I know who you are."

"You remember me?" Finn said, his heart swelling with hope.

"You were all over the internet, when it was still up and running. You're the dummy who tried to defeat the Plague. Didn't you get arrested?"

"Oh," Finn said, feeling suddenly defeated. "Do you know Julep?"

"No, and I'm not interested. Go beg for change some-where else."

Lincoln shut his window and pulled his curtains closed.

"I vote we leave him behind," Julep said.

"Me too," Highbeam added.

For a second, Finn agreed. This Lincoln was different—maybe too different. But he had to be certain his friend wasn't buried inside somewhere. He banged on the window and the curtains flew open. Lincoln's face was red and irritated.

"You're going to get my family in trouble," he scolded when he opened the window. "You are out past curfew. I'll call the Plague Guard."

"You would call the bugs on us? You lousy traitor!" Julep said. She looked like she might punch him in the nose, but Finn stepped between them.

"If you'll just hear me out. We used to be friends—" Finn didn't get to finish. Lincoln's window slammed shut again.

"This is fun," Highbeam said. "Kid, you told me we were going to find your dad, but we're just wasting time. We don't need this chump, unless your dad is being held hostage in a Broadway theater. Let's just leave him behind."

Finn pounded on the window again, but Lincoln didn't appear.

"I'm going to have to go in and get him," he said.

"You mean kidnap him?" Highbeam asked. "You've changed, little man."

"I'm not going to kidnap him," Finn mumbled.

"Dragging him out of his house against his will sounds like kidnapping to me," Julep said.

"I'd like to see you try."

Finn turned to find Lincoln standing behind them. The bigger kid bowed, then stepped into a fighting stance like he was the star of a kung fu movie.

"Okay, this is ridiculous. You don't know kung fu," Finn said.

"You're right. I know kalari," he said.

"What?"

"It's a martial art from India, dummy."

"Let me guess, you learned it for your college applications. Are you going to Ninja University?" Julep asked.

"Have you been stalking me? I told you to leave. You've given me no choice," Lincoln said.

"Listen, we didn't come here to fight," Finn said.

"Good." With a sudden twist, Lincoln's foot whistled through the air and slammed into Finn's jaw. The impact sent him and Highbeam's head tumbling to the ground. The robot fell facedown into the grass.

"This is the dumbest rescue mission of all time!" the robot grumbled.

"What's this?" Lincoln said, lifting the robot's head and peering into Highbeam's angry face.

"Stop dropping my head!"

Lincoln yelped and dropped the head back to the grass.

"Finn Foley, you have to do something," Julep said. "We're going to attract the bugs."

"I'm sorry, Lincoln, but you're coming with us," Finn said as he reached into his pack, snatched his sister's lunchbox, and felt the world tremble. Lightning exploded out of the lunchbox and a fresh wormhole appeared.

"What is that?" Lincoln cried, but before he got an answer, Finn shoved him into the portal and he vanished.

"So we're going with kidnapping. Fine by me," Julep said with a shrug, then leaped into the whirlpool after Lincoln.

"All right, buddy, next stop: the mother ship," Finn said to Highbeam as he scooped him off the grass.

"It's about time!" the robot grumbled. "And hey, can you get this leaf off my face?"

Finn sighed and jumped into the tear in space.

5

Lincoln's backyard turned into a long, hot, empty corridor glowing with red lights. It was dark and muggy, just like the last time Finn had visited the mother ship, which was designed to mimic the atmosphere of the Plague home world. The wormhole generator attached to his chest filled Finn's head with facts about every known world in the universe. From what he knew of the bug planet, it was a miserable place to live. No wonder the locusts spent all their time in space, looking for other worlds to capture and eat.

"What just happened?" Lincoln demanded. His face was flushed and angry, but his eyes were full of panic. He looked like he was about to punch Finn, but instead, he leaned over and barfed on the floor. Finn hid a smile. His Lincoln struggled with a delicate stomach, too. As gross as it was, at least the barf was familiar.

"We're on the Plague mother ship," Finn explained.

"What? Why? How?" Lincoln cried.

"That lunchbox is the coolest thing I have ever seen," Julep said.

"It opens shortcuts to pretty much anywhere in the universe I want to go," Finn said.

"That makes no sense! This can't be happening. We shouldn't be here. We're going to get captured. They'll kill us!" Lincoln snatched Finn by the collar and pulled him within an inch of his angry face. "Take us back right now!"

"All right, while he's having a fit, let's make a plan," said Highbeam. "I'd bet my paycheck the bugs have got Pre'at designing weapons, which means she's being held in a high-security wing of the ship. It would make a lot of sense to have the rest of me back together before we storm in there to get her."

"I totally agree. You got any idea in that computer brain of yours where they're keeping your body?" Finn asked.

"I've got a map of the whole ship!" the robot cheered. "My partner, Dax, and I infiltrated this place when we were spies. Follow me."

Before they could take a single step, a team of bug soldiers marched toward them from the far end of the corridor. In a panic, Finn opened a nearby door and pushed everyone inside.

"This is insane!" Lincoln cried. His voice was high, and he was breathing hard. "I'm going to die on an alien spaceship. All the work I've done, the tutors, the test prep, the study groups—all of it was for nothing!"

"Shhhh! They'll hear you whining all the way down the hall," Julep said as she clamped her hand on Lincoln's mouth.

Finn pressed his ear to the door to listen for footsteps. Had the bugs seen them? Were they going to burst into the room any second? His heart felt like it was going to beat out of his chest.

"Wait! What's this?" Lincoln asked, pulling away from Julep.

Finn scanned the room for the first time. It was small and dark, with a dim red light hanging overhead that made everything creepy. In the center sat a sturdy table with a glass container on top, and the walls were lined with steel cabinets. The room had a strange chemical smell that bit at his nose.

Julep stepped up to the table. The glass container was long and cylindrical. Inside was a shadowy form about as tall as a full-grown man. Unfortunately, the room's lighting prevented Finn from getting a closer look.

"Is that a person?" Julep asked.

"Awww, man," Lincoln complained.

"Don't touch anything," Highbeam said. "Let's just wait for the soldiers to pass and then get out of here."

If Julep heard him, she ignored his warnings. Her fingers found a panel of buttons on the surface of the glass, and before anyone could stop her, she pressed one. The glass case vanished in a cloud of mist and the figure beneath was revealed. It was not human. Its skin was gray, and it had long, thin limbs. The face was missing eyes, but Finn found them on the palms of the creature's hands. Finn gasped. He recognized this alien. They'd met several times before.

"Miles Teague!" Highbeam cried as his face icons morphed from shock to sadness.

"You know this thing?" Lincoln asked.

"He's not a thing," Highbeam snapped. This is Commander Miles Teague, a freedom fighter and one of the greatest leaders the universe has ever known. He founded the interplanetary resistance to fight the Plague. He was my hero."

Finn wasn't sure how to respond. Highbeam's grief came as a surprise. The story the robot told didn't sound at all like the one Finn had lived through. In his timeline, Finn, Highbeam, and his friends had turned to Teague for help with the wormhole generator, but Teague and the rest of his council had betrayed them. The commander tricked Pre'at into building a second wormhole generator, which he gave to the Plague in exchange for a promise of peace. The bugs agreed to leave Nemeth alone, but unfortunately, the machine allowed them to find Earth. Teague knew what would happen, but he didn't care.

Clearly, things had unfolded differently in this timeline. Just another example of how the changes Finn made in the past affected the present. If Teague wasn't a traitor in this timeline, the Plague had managed to find their way to Earth some other way. Someone had still given them the wormhole technology.

"Um . . . there's something crawling out of him," Lincoln said, pointing to the folds of Teague's purple robes. A tiny creature was digging its way out of the sleeve. When it finally freed itself, Finn saw a baby locust.

"Uh-oh." Highbeam's sad expression morphed from grief to alarm. "Which button did you press, Julep?"

"I don't know. Why?"

"Push it again. Push them all! We have to put Teague back in his box!" the robot cried.

"Why?"

"Bugs lay their eggs inside of bodies until they hatch," the robot explained.

"So what?" Lincoln said. "It's just one bug."

"It's not just one. It's one of thousands," Highbeam said.

More tiny locust hoppers clawed their way out of

Teague's clothes. One became a dozen; then a dozen became a hundred. Soon there were more than Finn could count, and they were hopping around the room. He stepped up next to Julep, hoping to find a key panel to close the glass shield, but none of the buttons made sense.

A waterfall of bugs spilled onto the floor. Many of them buzzed around Finn, Lincoln, and Julep, screeching and clicking their back legs together. They flew into the kids' faces and hair. Finn swatted at them, but there were too many.

"We have to get out of here," Highbeam said.

Finn could barely see the robot's head through the swarm, only the faint glow of his face. He snatched at it blindly and stuffed it under his arm. Shouting for Lincoln and Julep to follow, he pushed the door open and the group tumbled into the hallway. Together they forced the door shut, then helped one another slap away the bugs still clinging to them. The baby locusts quickly recovered and flew en masse down the corridor.

"I don't like this place!" Lincoln cried as he hopped up and down, shivering.

"We have to keep moving. The babies will warn the adults," Highbeam said.

"Just a sec." Julep took off her pack and reached inside. Finn expected her to pull out one of her strange books—she carried a personal library of everything from parallel worlds to chupacabras everywhere she went. As happy as he was to see another of her familiar habits, now was a lousy time to do research.

"Julep, your books can wait," he said.

"Books?" she said as she removed a peach-sized metal sphere. It had a bright red button on the side.

"Whoa! Where did you get a sonic grenade?" Highbeam asked.

"I stole it. I'm the Mongoose, remember?" she said.

"You're the Mongoose?" Lincoln cried. "You're a criminal."

"A criminal?" Julep cried. "I'm trying to save the world, dude!"

"You're causing trouble, which only makes the bugs angry. If it wasn't for you, there would be a lot fewer patrols and house searches," Lincoln said, standing his ground.

Julep looked like she was ready to throw her grenade at him, but Finn intervened.

"What do you plan to do with that?"

"I'm going to throw one inside that incubation room so the little bugs don't grow up to be big, world-conquering bugs," she explained. "Do all these rooms have hoppers in them? I have more grenades. We can take them all out at once."

"We didn't come here to blow up bugs," Finn said.

"Maybe you didn't, but I did. The Plague is going to destroy our world. If we have a chance to make it harder for them, we should take it," she argued.

"Listen, your plan might wipe out a generation of bugs, but it will set off alarms and get us caught. My plan means the bugs never show up on Earth at all. You have to trust me," Finn said.

Julep's jaw was set and her expression determined. Finn had never thought of her as stubborn. In fact, she was always the one he could count on to be level-headed.

"He's right. Save the grenades," Highbeam said. "A ruckus is only going to draw their attention. You don't want to end up on one of those tables with bugs crawling out of you, right?"

Julep slowly put the grenade back into her pack.

"Fine, for now," she grumbled, "but if I get a chance to do some damage, I'm going to take it, plan or no plan."

"Let's keep moving," Finn said, hurrying back down the hall and hoping she wouldn't change her mind.

"We had to bring them, huh?" Highbeam whispered.

Finn bit his lip. He was starting to wonder if he had made a terrible mistake.

Highbeam called out directions through the labyrinth of hallways, and Finn followed his instructions. Finally, they came to a door and he pushed it open. On the other side he found a catwalk so high above the floor that it made him dizzy. Through filth and fog, he could make out a glowing red light below them. The noise down there was deafening, and the heat was so intense it roasted his face. He knew this catwalk. He had been on one just like it before. It spanned the length of the room, breaking off into other catwalks. Far below, the mother ship's engines roared.

"Is there somewhere on this ship that isn't hot?" Lincoln asked.

"The way you three squabble, I figured we were better off staying out of sight," Highbeam explained. "This is the bugs' least favorite part of their ship. Working in the engine room is considered a punishment. There won't be many soldiers to get in our way."

"I can guess why," Julep said. "It smells like the junk they put in their hoverbike tanks. Ugh."

"It also has the most direct route to the robotics lab. Take those stairs over there," the robot said. His icons formed an arrow that pointed to the right.

They scaled five flights until their legs were burning. At the top was a service door. Finn was about to push it open, but Highbeam stopped him.

"Whoa! The armory is on the other side. It's one of the most heavily guarded levels on the ship."

"Armory?" Julep asked, her curiosity turned up to ten.

"Don't even think about it, kid," Highbeam said.

"If we can't go through the door, then why did we take this route?" Finn asked.

"'Cause we're using the shortcut through the ventilation system," the robot explained.

"That sounds dangerous," Lincoln said. "And dirty."

"The access panel is at the top of that ladder behind you," Highbeam said.

Finn climbed the ladder and found the panel just as Highbeam said he would. He turned a handle and gave the door a yank. It swung open, releasing a cloud of dust and revealing a space just big enough for him to crawl into.

"You first, buddy," Finn said. He placed Highbeam's head in the shaft and the robot's face lit up the dark, cramped space. Finn crawled in behind him.

Julep was next, but after a moment Finn felt her tugging on his jeans.

"Lincoln's not coming," she said. "It's the jacket. He says he doesn't want to get it dirty."

"Aaargh! Leave him," Highbeam said. "He hasn't stopped complaining since we got here. He acts like he's the only person who's ever been kidnapped and taken to an alien spaceship!"

"We can't just leave him," Finn said. "I'll go back."

It was a tight squeeze, but Finn and Julep switched places. Soon Finn's head was sticking out the ventilation door. Lincoln was below, sitting on the catwalk with his arms crossed in defiance.

"Is this really the best time to put your foot down?" Finn said.

"Go on without me. You can come back once you've done whatever it is you're doing here," Lincoln said. "I can't get this blazer dirty."

"It's a school uniform!" Finn cried.

"It's more than a school uniform! It's from the Hudson Valley Preparatory Academy for the Gifted!" he said. "It represents pride, respect, and scholastic achievement. The students who go there grow up to steer the course of history! I swore an oath to protect this crest."

Finn fought the urge to laugh. Lincoln Sidana, a kid who'd once worn a bathrobe to school as a jacket, who sometimes showed up wearing mismatched shoes and proudly bragged about how few pairs of underwear he owned, was being fancy about an ugly green suit jacket with a bird sewn onto it. Still, Finn could tell mocking the kid was not going to motivate him. He needed to try a different approach.

"Listen, I know you don't remember me, but we used to be best friends. You're smart, quick on your feet, and brave. I brought you with us because in the past you were always there to help me solve problems, and right now, I need you more than ever."

Lincoln huffed for a few moments, then stood and brushed the dust off his shorts.

"Well, fine, then," Lincoln said, and he climbed the ladder.

"You won't regret this, Lincoln," Finn said. "When all is said and done, you are going to be a hero and a legend. If you want something for your college essay, I don't think you can do any better than how you saved the world."

"It better not be dirty up there," he said.

"It's spotless," Finn lied.

"You're lying," Lincoln said.

"Just a little."

"I've only known you fifteen minutes and every second of it has been the worst," Lincoln said.

Finn made room for him inside the ventilation shaft, and the group crawled through the passage with Highbeam's bright face pushing through the darkness. The space was blisteringly hot, and there seemed to be endless turns. As he sweated through his shirt, Finn quietly wondered if Highbeam was lost, but the robot kept urging them onward. Soon they moved into a cooler section of the ship. Finn guessed that they were no longer directly over the engine room.

"I think we're there," Highbeam announced as they approached another vent. "Point my noggin downward so I can see."

Finn did as he was asked.

"Oh, sweet baby!" the robot continued. "My beautiful body is down there, and it's all in one piece. Thank the stars! Do you know how long it takes to order a replacement? Years, sometimes even decades! Customer service at the robot factory is a nightmare."

Finn peeked through the slats and saw the body, too. It was standing against a wall in a lab. Other robots were scattered around the room, as was a collection of metal body parts.

"Is it safe to go get it?" Finn asked.

"There's not a bug in sight," Highbeam said.

Finn carefully opened the vent door. He handed Highbeam's head back to Julep and slowly lowered himself as far as he could. The fall was roughly six feet, but he managed it without any injuries. As he was getting his bearings, something heavy fell on his head. It was Julep's backpack. His bruised skull told him there was more than one sonic grenade inside it.

Julep herself followed, then Highbeam's head, and finally Lincoln, who landed with the grace of a cat.

"There better not be any dead aliens in here," he said.

Finn scanned the room to get a better look. Mechanical torsos, legs, arms, and robot parts were on tables, stuffed in cans, and hanging out of drawers. Some of the robot bodies were short and squat, while others were big and bulky. A few had tank treads instead of feet. The wiring in some spilled out of their bellies and onto the floor.

"This is a house of horrors!" Highbeam yelped. "Oh, the depravity! C'mon, body. Let's get out of here. I can't imagine what you've seen."

The robot's face icons swam across the glass, and suddenly, his headless body lumbered forward, its arms outstretched. Finn reached Highbeam's head out to it, but the torso walked past him to another table. There, it snatched another head, this one both strange and buglike. It had huge eyes, a snapping mandible, and antennas sticking out of the top. It looked like a robotic locust. Highbeam's body forced it between its shoulder blades, gave it a good twist, and turned toward the group with fiery red eyes. The robot's legs rubbed together as if they were trying to make a click. Instead, they sprayed sparks around the room.

"Um, what's going on?" Finn asked.

"My body is cheating on me with another head!" Highbeam cried. "Body, how could you? Hang on! I'm sending a signal to reject the new part."

There was a loud *ding*. The body reached up, yanked off the new bug head, and slammed it down on the table. It snatched Highbeam's noggin just as quickly and forced it into place. His computer-screen face lit up with fireworks and waving flags.

"That's better," he said, shaking himself like a wet dog. "Now let's go find Pre'at before—"

Ding!

Suddenly, Highbeam's hands were yanking his head off his neck. Before anyone could react, the bug head was back in control.

"You've gotta be kidding me!" Highbeam cried from the spot on the table where his body had dropped him.

"Um, can I help?" Finn asked.

"I got this!" Highbeam growled.

Ding! The bug head was unscrewed once more. This time, Highbeam kicked it across the room, where it crashed against a wall. "This is my body! Go find your own."

Finn half-expected to hear a *ding,* and another struggle for control, but the booted bug head stayed put in the corner of the room. He assumed it was broken.

"All right, let's never speak of this again," Highbeam said once his head was comfortably back in place.

"Um, do all robot heads do that?" Lincoln said as he pointed toward the alien head. Four spindly legs poked out of either side. Without warning it sprang at Highbeam, clamping its metallic talons onto his face.

"What in the devil?" Highbeam shouted as he struggled to pull it off.

"I think you made it mad," Julep said.

Finn snatched a hammer off a table. He hopped

around, waiting for just the right opportunity to hit the evil head, but as soon as he saw one, it attacked from another angle.

Finally, Highbeam threw it to the ground, snatched the hammer out of Finn's hand, and smacked it over and over again.

"Stay. Down. You. Ugly. Cuss!" he cried with each angry blow. Finally, the machine's red eyes turned black and all the fight went out of it. Highbeam hovered, panting, even though Finn was sure he didn't actually breathe air. "There! I killed it. I killed the evil head."

That was when it started to hum, as if fueled by revenge. The number ten appeared in one of its cracked eyeballs. It turned into a nine, and then an eight. Finn knew what a countdown meant, and it wasn't good.

"All right, everybody out!" he cried, and the group dashed into the hall. While everyone tried to calm themselves, Highbeam broke into giggles.

"Ornery thing, wasn't it?" Highbeam asked.

"This isn't funny," Lincoln said. "There is nothing funny about this at all."

A huge explosion blew the door off its hinges and smoke billowed into the hallway. An alarm mashed Finn's ears and flashing emergency lights dazzled his eyes.

"Well, if they didn't know we were here before, they do now," Julep said.

"C'mon!" Highbeam dragged the kids around a corner and into the path of a team of bug soldiers.

"Hey! Stop!" they shouted.

The group doubled back. Sonic blasts whizzed past them, but the smoke prevented the Plague soldiers from getting a good shot. Highbeam led the children through a junction, around a corner, and down a new corridor with the sound of angry soldiers in pursuit.

"Where are you taking us?" Finn asked.

"Here!" the robot said, shoving them through a doorway. Finn found himself in a laboratory far bigger than any they had seen so far. Standing in the middle of hundreds of bubbling and hissing experiments was Pre'at, four hundred pounds of pasty, sweaty, eyeball-covered genius.

Lincoln whispered, "Dude." His face was a perfect blend of shock and fear.

Julep yelped, took out her phone, and captured some pictures of the alien scientist.

"Well, if it isn't Finn Foley," Pre'at said when she looked up from her work. "I suppose you've come to rescue me."

"We did," Highbeam said. He raced around the room snatching furniture and shoving it against the door.

On the other side, the bugs were pounding and firing weapons in a frenzied effort to get at the heroes. "And if you don't mind, we'd like to make it quick."

"You've made a terrible mistake," Pre'at said. In her hand was a shock blaster, aimed right at Finn. "I have no intention of going anywhere with you."

6

"The mashed-potato lady is pointing a weapon at us," Lincoln said.

"Pre'at? I thought you were on our side," Finn cried.

"The only side I'm on is my own," the scientist said. "I tried the hero route with you and look where it got me—stuck on this smelly ship. I'm lucky to be alive. Why would I join your losing cause again?"

"Because it's the right thing to do!" Highbeam said. "We took an oath to the resistance to fight the bugs. Now you've joined them?"

"I have done nothing of the sort! I started my own resistance, right here in this lab. The weapons the bugs are forcing me to build are sabotaged. Everything will backfire and bring their ultimate defeat. I should have put all my faith in my brain at the start."

"Are all aliens this arrogant?" Julep asked.

"She's actually being humble right now," Finn admitted. "Pre'at, we didn't come here to wreck your plans. If you want to stay and beat them from the inside, go for it, but I still need your help. You're the only person smart enough to solve my problem."

"I suppose you think flattery will change my mind?" the Alcherian asked.

"It always did before," Highbeam mumbled. "And if not, then do it for Alcheria. Have you forgotten what the bugs did to your home world?"

Pre'at rolled all of her eyes, but she set her weapon down on the tabletop.

"What do you want, Earthboy?"

"I need you to send us to the subatomic," Finn told her.

"The subatomic?"

"Yes, it's this tiny place—"

"I know what the subatomic is, child!" Pre'at snapped. "Why do you want to go there?"

"I'm looking for my dad. I'm told he's on a speck of dust underneath my thumbnail."

"Just so we're clear, I'm not going with them," Lincoln said. "I have school tomorrow."

"They shut all the schools down the day the Plague invaded," Julep reminded him.

"I have online tutors," Lincoln cried. "An alien attack is no excuse to let your education suffer."

"Finn, I am a genius with an unmatched intellect, but what you're asking is beyond even me. No one has figured out how to reach the subatomic," Pre'at said.

"Someone has, just not yet." He opened his palm and said, "Sticky," to activate the futuristic technology he'd found in the twenty-sixth century, happy to find that it was not erased by the new timeline. A hologram of yellow paper appeared above his hand.

Pre'at's hundred eyeballs widened with surprise.

"Fascinating," she said as a collection of magnifying lenses slid out of her clothing and over her eyeballs. She studied the glowing paper with great intensity.

"It stores information on the subatomic level," he said. "A future version of me figured out how to adapt it so that a person could be sent there as well. My dad has been stuck in it for a year and a half."

"It's incredible! Do you know what I could do with something like this?" Pre'at said to Finn. "I could hide weapons, even whole armies. Why, I could shrink the entire mother ship."

"Can we hurry this up? We're going to be knee-deep in locusts any second now," Highbeam said. He pressed his shoulder against the door to hold back the bugs fighting to enter from the other side. "Hey, whiny and weirdo, how about a little help?"

"That's not cool," Julep said.

Lincoln and Julep rushed to help, though they both complained about their nicknames.

"Inspiration cannot be rushed," Pre'at said. She scooped up a strange tool from her desk and hurried over to the door. A blue flame shot out of its tip, a lot like a welding torch, but instead of heating up the metal, it froze the door in a thick layer or ice.

"That will buy us a little time," she said.

"You had that all along?" Highbeam growled.

"I have a lot on my mind, robot!" Pre'at said, dismissing him with a wave of her sweaty hand. She rushed back to her desk, where Finn was waiting. "Now, about this machine you want me to build. You realize it's impossible."

Finn's heart sank with disappointment.

"I mean, not for me. I'm brilliant," she continued. "Unfortunately, there is a very practical problem: How do I power a machine that can shrink people? The amount of energy needed would be immense, even more than for this ship's engines, I'm afraid. We'd need something like—"

"How about a machine that opens wormholes?" Finn said as he slipped off his backpack. A second later, he plopped the pink unicorn lunchbox on the desk.

"Grrr, I hoped I'd never see that infernal thing again. Nevertheless, I'm afraid even it isn't enough," Pre'at said.

"Wait!" Finn dug into the backpack and found his father's time-travel lasso. He set it in Pre'at's hands.

"A rope?" she asked.

"Not exactly. It's a time machine."

"That's ridiculous."

"I have a lunchbox that opens tunnels in space, but a time-travel lasso is too much for you to accept?"

"Good point." Pre'at squinted through her magnifying lenses at the rope.

"Earthboy, you have the most interesting technology," Pre'at remarked. "I had a colleague back home who claimed he was building a time machine. One day I went into the lab and he and his gadget were gone. No one ever heard from him again."

"Pre'at, I need you to focus," Finn said. The noises outside the door were getting louder. "What if you combine the lunchbox and the lasso? Will that give you enough power to send us to the subatomic?"

"There's only one way to find out. I need some space," she said as she cleared a worktable with an unforgiving swipe of her arm, leaving only the lunchbox and the lasso. Finn watched as she pried and poked at the devices. For such a slow, lumbering creature, Pre'at's hands moved like lightning.

"They're burning through the steel," Highbeam said. A red dot appeared in the center of the door and was quickly growing in size.

"I have an excellent idea, Foley," Lincoln said. "Take me home, where it's safe. You can come back and wait for the eyeball lady to make your machine."

"Yeah, I think he's right," Julep said as she eyed the door.

"I only need a few moments more," the scientist said.

"You know that monsters are going to get us, right?"

Highbeam rushed across the room, snatched Pre'at's sonic blaster off the floor, and shoved it into Julep's hands.

"Then let's make sure they don't get the chance. Have you ever used one of these before?" he asked.

Julep nodded and pointed it toward the door.

"Hey, where's my laser gun?" Lincoln asked.

"Use your karate on them," Julep said.

"It's not karate! It's kalari! It's one of the oldest martial arts in the world."

"Then kalari them in the face, kid," Highbeam said. "Unless you don't want to get your fancy jacket dirty. Activate Demolition Mode!"

A yellow warning light flashed on his steel chest. Steam escaped from his hips and joints, and his head sank into his upper torso. An alarm sounded, and his arms started to swing in wide loops, faster and faster, until they were a blur.

"Boy, hand me a roll of Caltervian film from the rack," Pre'at said, pointing to a pile of supplies nearby. Finn rushed to it, sorting through everything but not having a clue what Caltervian film looked like. Finally, he found a roll of bright blue tarp and held it up.

"Is this it?"

"Of course it is," Pre'at said. "Don't be a moron."

He rushed back to her and the scientist snatched it without so much as a thank-you. He watched her lift the lunchbox and the lasso, then unroll the film onto her empty desktop.

"Here they come!" Julep cried. The red spot on the door was now as big as a manhole cover.

"It's now or never!" Highbeam roared.

"Can everyone be quiet? How am I supposed to do the impossible with all this noise?" Pre'at complained as she connected the lasso and the lunchbox with wires and clamps. When she was finished, she set the devices on top of the blue tarp. Finn watched them sink into it like pennies in a pool, vanishing, while the tarp stayed thin and blue. The lights in the lab suddenly dimmed. Finn heard the ship's engines whining to a stop before rumbling back to life. There was even a crackle and pop of circuity inside the alien technology fused to his chest. "It's ready. I just need you to sign a waiver acknowledging that you are testing a new technology and that any number of disasters could occur, including loss of life or limb due to fire, melting, vaporizing, imploding, spontaneous combustion—"

"Pre'at! Turn it on!" Highbeam shouted over his swinging arms.

"Fine, but if parts of the boy shrink and the rest stay the same size, I don't want to hear any whining," she cried.

Pop! The circle in the center of the door opened. Through it, Finn could see movement. There were bugs on the other side. A big black eye peered through the hole at them.

"Finn Foley!" a voice said. To Finn, almost all the bugs sounded the same, but this was a voice he knew very, very well. It belonged to the worst of them.

He gasped. "Sin Kraven."

"When I get through this door I'm going to tear you limb from limb," Kraven said.

Sin Kraven was the ugliest of the locusts and a member of an elite military branch known as the Plague High Guard. Finn remembered him arriving on Earth through the lunchbox, then causing havoc all over Cold Spring. The bug's mission was to retrieve the wormhole technology and kill Finn in the process. To do it, he had kidnapped Mr. Doogan, Finn's school principal, and dragged the poor man through town. Doogan ultimately stopped Kraven's plans, but the bug turned the tables on everyone. He returned to his people to point them toward Earth. Luckily, Finn used their own wormhole generator to send them to a part of space so far away they would never find their way back to Earth again. Unfortunately, he and his friends messed with the timeline, so now it had never happened, and Kraven was back to cause trouble.

"I don't know how you escaped your cell, pinkskin, but I promise that you will soon wish you had stayed there," Kraven growled through the hole in the door.

"Friend of yours?" Julep asked.

"His name is Kraven," Finn explained. "He doesn't like me very much."

"Welcome to the club," Lincoln said.

"Pre'at, is your gizmo ready?" Highbeam said, his body returning to normal.

The scientist yanked the tarp off the table and spread it flat on the floor. It was long and narrow, and when Finn looked closely, he noticed that its surface was wet, as if it were connected to a garden hose. Only, there was no hose. Finn couldn't tell where the water was coming from.

"What is this?" Lincoln asked.

"It's a slide, of course," Pre'at said. "You can't just step into the subatomic. You need to build up a little speed."

"It's a slip-and-slide," Julep said.

"A subatomic slip-and-slide!" Finn cheered.

"The instructions are so simple a human can understand them. First you run, then you dive, and the machine does the rest."

A shock blast came through the hole in the door and

rattled the room. It hit an unfinished invention and set it ablaze.

"That was important!" Pre'at raged. "Get going before they destroy everything I've created!"

"Who's first?" Highbeam asked.

"I got this." Julep secured her backpack across her shoulders and without a word sprinted forward. Finn marveled at her fearlessness. Julep was always brave, but this was next level. When she reached the edge of the tarp, she dove, hit the wet plastic, and whizzed toward the end of the sheet, laughing all the way. "Whoo-hoo!"

As she went, she got smaller and smaller. By the time she reached the other end of the slide, she had vanished altogether.

"Lincoln, it's your turn," Finn said.

"No way! I'm not doing that," Lincoln said.

"You have to," Finn cried. His Lincoln was always eager to try out new technology—he loved anything with buttons and lights, especially if it blew up—but this Lincoln . . . he was a coward.

"I've had enough of your jibber-jabber," Highbeam growled. He snatched Lincoln by the back of his blazer and tossed him onto the slide. The boy hit the tarp with a pained "Oof!" He flopped and struggled, shrinking all the while. Soon he was gone, just like Julep.

Highbeam turned to Finn. "Sorry, but he's annoying. You're next, little man!"

"Thank you!" Finn said to Pre'at.

"I do what I can," she replied. "I hope whatever you intend to do in the subatomic helps destroy the Plague. I'm a genius, but I can't do it all on my own."

Finn eyed the tarp. He once had a real slip-and-slide when he was little. It was probably his favorite toy of all time. He and Kate spent hours on it in their backyard. So, with a smile on his face, he rushed forward and dove. Unfortunately, the floor was a lot harder than his lawn and the water was ice-cold. The sensation of shrinking was unnerving, too. As he got closer and closer to the end of the slide, the world got bigger and bigger, until it stopped making sense. Pre'at, who was once just a few inches taller than him, now looked like a mountain. In fact, everything around him was enormous. He wondered if they had made a terrible mistake, but it was too late. Everything went black.

The door of the lab blew off its hinges and steel flew in every direction. It was a miracle Pre'at and Highbeam weren't injured. A dozen bug soldiers rushed into the room, their sonic cannons primed and ready.

"Go!" Pre'at shouted at the robot. "You won't get another chance."

Highbeam didn't hesitate. He sprinted toward the slip-and-slide.

"Stop him!" Kraven said as he charged through the door. His wings extended and he leaped, soaring across the room and crashing into Highbeam. The impact sent them both skidding along the wet, slippery surface. They struggled for dominance, trading punches while inching closer and closer to the end of the tarp. With each brutal attack, the duo shrank. Soon they looked like two action figures come to life. Kraven's dumbfounded troops watched in stunned silence until their leader and the robot blinked out of existence.

"After them!" one of the soldiers shouted, but before the bugs could follow, the slip-and-slide rolled itself up and vanished into thin air.

Finn plummeted into nothing. He remembered *Alice's Adventures in Wonderland,* the story of a girl who tumbled into a hole that led to a magical world. He had always hated that story, but if the worst that happened was that he woke up with a Cheshire cat staring at him, he'd thank his lucky stars. The strange sensation of shrinking was odd and unsettling, as if he were a balloon with a tiny hole that couldn't hold any air. And the world around him was changing, too. At first it was so dark he couldn't see his hand in front of his face, but then a brilliant white light appeared beneath him. It started as a pinprick, then swallowed him whole, and when he came out the other side, he was in a void surrounded by tiny moving dots. As they got bigger, he saw that they were alive with wild colors and shapes. Some had spikes and tails, while others looked like hairy fingers. When they were small, they seemed harmless, but it wasn't long before those spikes got sharper and vicious. One of the creatures wrapped its sticky tail around Finn's waist and tried to pull him into its gooey body. If he hadn't shrunk, he was sure he would have been absorbed. He worried his friends might have been eaten, too.

"Julep! Lincoln! Highbeam!" he cried, but no one answered.

Suddenly, the creatures were gone, replaced by little balls of electricity orbiting his body. They raced to him from every direction, joining the others in an invisible chain. He vaguely remembered something about the makeup of molecules from science class. Was he part of an element? Mrs. Long would probably give him extra credit if he told her this story.

As the balls of energy got bigger, they pressed against him, threatening to crush his tiny body. Just when he was sure he was about to be pulverized, another light appeared below, swirling like the wormholes that came out of the lunchbox. It pulled at him with invisible hands, yanking him away from the atoms and into its void. The colors around him changed from white to red to blue to green to pink to yellow to orange: an entire rainbow of dizzying beauty and terror. As it dragged him in, he reached out, hoping to find something to cling to that would stop his descent, but there was nothing to hang on to. He was helpless, and the light devoured him.

All sound stopped. He couldn't tell if he was falling or floating or shrinking anymore. All he knew for certain was that he felt a rush of cool air underneath him. He saw a dark sky full of stars and moons. And then there was a thump.

8

The light behind his eyelids demanded attention. When he blinked them open, he saw a huge silver orb high above him, with four smaller glowing satellites circling it. The sky was a swirl of purples, reds, oranges, and pinks, the way the Hudson Valley horizon looked during a sunset, and everything smelled clean and crisp, the way it does after a fresh snow. He sat up and found himself lying in a bed of tall bluish-green grass that spread out in every direction. It swayed back and forth in a warm breeze that would have been comforting if not for the ache in every single one of his muscles. The last time he had hurt this bad was when he'd fallen out of the pine tree in his backyard.

"My body is broken," Lincoln groaned from somewhere nearby. "Even my earlobes hurt."

Finn gazed around until he located his friend. Lincoln was flat on his back a few yards away.

"Where are we?" Lincoln asked as he slowly got to his feet. He seemed woozy and unbalanced.

"I think we're here," Finn said.

Without warning, Lincoln leaped on top of him and knocked him back to the ground. He sat on top of Finn with his fists clenched, just inches from Finn's face.

"Where is 'here'?"

"The subatomic."

"Like that's supposed to explain something! Why are you doing this to me? I didn't want to come with you. I don't even know you."

"Yes you do!" Finn cried. "You just need to look at the phone!"

"What phone?"

Finn reached into his pocket and took out Julep's phone. He pressed the on button several times, but nothing happened.

"It's dead! Maybe coming here zapped its battery," he said. "There are pictures of us on it. If I could charge it, I could prove that what I'm telling you is true. You're my best friend."

He stared up into the Lincoln's angry face, hoping to see some flicker of memory, a door creaking open to release a memory, but there was only suspicion and anger. This Lincoln wasn't Finn's. He didn't dress like

Finn's Lincoln, he didn't talk like him, and he probably didn't have any of the qualities Finn was counting on to find his dad. His Lincoln was brave and tough and quick on his feet. This Lincoln was a coward, fussy, and a complainer. Bringing him to the subatomic suddenly felt like the dumbest idea ever.

"Is this the same stupid story you told that girl?" Lincoln demanded.

"That girl"! Where was Julep? Finn shoved the boy off and clambered to his feet. Where was was Highbeam? He scanned the field in every direction, shouting their names and hearing only his voice echo in the distance.

"I don't see them," Finn said.

"They're around here somewhere. What's important is that we find that slip-and-slide," Lincoln said. "I assume we need it to get back home?"

Finn nodded.

Lincoln shook his fist at him and roared like an angry lion. He stomped through the grass, looking for the blue tarp. He didn't seem at all worried about Julep or Highbeam. Finn left him to his search and kept looking for the others. Where could they be? The grass was so tall it was quite possible that they were lying unconscious nearby, hidden from his view. It was also possible that he and Lincoln had been knocked out after the fall for a long time and that Julep and Highbeam had woken, couldn't find them, and had given up. But where would they go? Aside from some low black hills in the distance, all Finn saw was grass and a few skinny trees.

"Hey, what's that?" Lincoln said.

Something stirred in the brush about fifty yards away. It moved in their direction, parting the grass as it came closer.

"Julep?" Finn shouted. "Is that you?"

If it was Julep, she didn't answer. Why was she crouching so low, trying to stay out of sight? And wait: there was something else, a few feet to the right, scurrying toward them, too. Was that Highbeam? It couldn't be. The robot was seven feet tall. He couldn't hide in the brush even if he tried.

"I don't like this," Finn said.

Lincoln gestured to his right, where two more figures were bending the grass as they slinked closer. When Finn looked to the left, he saw even more. There was movement all around them. In fact, the boys were completely surrounded.

"Whatever you want, you better think twice! I was junior champion at the Hudson Valley Martial Arts Expo last year," Lincoln shouted.

Suddenly, a girl about their age rose out of the grass. She had dark-brown skin and hair that hung in thick, floppy ropes down to her shoulders. Her clothes were dusty and covered with patches, and she had blue paint spread across both her cheeks. She carried a slingshot in one hand and a white stone in the other. She loaded it into her weapon and aimed it at Lincoln's head.

"I know how to fight, too," she said.

Another child stood up next to her, followed by another, and another, all as filthy as the first, and all sporting the same blue paint on their faces. Each was armed with a different weapon: a club, a spear, a sword, even something that looked like a garden rake. A round-faced boy wearing a black velvet top hat inserted a rock into a leather sling and spun it like a pinwheel.

"We don't want any trouble," Finn said.

"Unfortunately, you've found some," the girl said.

"The grasslands belong to the Runaways, and there is a price for crossing without permission," the boy in the top hat said.

"How much does it cost?" Finn asked.

"Trust me, kid," the girl said. "You can't afford it."

9

Before the boys could stop them, the children bound Finn's and Lincoln's hands behind their backs and prodded them through the grass with pointy spears. Lincoln groused and complained with every step, demanding to be released and threatening to have his father file a lawsuit against their captors. Finn tried to tune him out and instead studied their kidnappers' every move. Most of them were young, seven or eight years old, except for the boy in the top hat, who seemed to be closer to thirteen, and the girl, who seemed to be their age. She spent much of the walk eyeing the horizon, as if concerned that something or someone might be watching them.

It was a long walk. The landscape was breathtaking. The black hills shone like mounds of precious jewels.

The sky was more lavender than blue, and strange birds whirled in it. They seemed to be made of pulsating light. At first Finn thought he was imagining them, but when something darted across their path sparkling with the same energy, he realized they weren't illusions. As they walked, he saw more and more signs of life, and all of them were made of an electrical charge, like animal-shaped bolts of lightning. They boggled his mind.

"Where are you taking us?" Lincoln demanded.

"Shut up, spy," the girl said.

"We're not spies," Finn said.

"I'm not even with him. He kidnapped me," Lincoln said.

"Lying is a crime," the boy in the top hat said. "We may have to torture you now. Isn't that right, Rabbit?"

"It's a very serious crime, Nico," the girl said, flashing Finn a steely expression. "Did Proton send you? Are there more of you?"

"Who's Proton?" Lincoln asked.

"The first mistake you made was coming here. The second is assuming we're dumb," she said.

"He's not assuming anything. No one sent us here," Finn said. He stepped between Rabbit and Lincoln, hoping to defuse the tension. "My name is Finn and this is Lincoln. We came here with—"

Lincoln kicked him in the shin so hard his eyes watered. There were kinder ways to tell him to shut up, but he got the point. These kids didn't need to know about Julep and Highbeam.

Rabbit reached into her pocket, took out two bandanas, and stuffed one into each of their mouths.

"I'm tired of hearing your lies," she said.

They trekked onward. Soon the ground sloped downward into a valley. At the bottom was a nearly dry riverbed with a narrow stream snaking through dust and rocks. As the Runaways followed the stream, they seemed to share Rabbit's paranoia. They studied the hills and the sky, as if someone or something might leap down and tear them apart. Finn scanned his surroundings. If something was out there, he and Lincoln didn't have a chance.

The group continued until they reached the mouth of a cave. The interior was completely dark, but that didn't intimidate their captors. Rabbit held up her hand and nearly all the children, including Nico, darted into the blackness. Only a couple stayed behind. They seemed to have the pointiest weapons.

Lincoln grumbled through his gag. Rabbit ignored him, and they stood silently waiting in the hot suns. After several minutes, Nico returned.

"It's clear," he said.

Finn and Lincoln were shoved forward into pitch blackness. They stumbled over rocks that rolled away beneath their feet. Just when Finn was sure he would fall and hurt himself, he realized the cave wasn't as dark as before. Minerals in the stone walls glowed luminescent green, offering a faint light. They exposed a path that ran along a stream. Rabbit led the way, making several sharp turns that took them deeper into the cave. At times the passage grew so narrow everyone had to squeeze through one by one. Eventually, they came to a dead stop in front of a wall of thick black vines. Rabbit and Nico brushed them aside and urged the boys farther. Beyond was an underground lagoon of shimmering electric-blue water. In the middle of the pool, a huge structure of vines and bamboo poles stood nearly three stories high. It consisted of huts linked by crude wooden bridges. Each hut was small, only large enough for one or two people. More children peered out their open doors or from the water, where they hefted baskets of sparkly red and green fish. Finn tried to count the children, but there were too many.

Rabbit removed their gags, then blasted a shrill whistle. All the children stopped what they were doing and raced to meet her. Some swung effortlessly down to the beach from vines tied to the huts, while others dove into the water and climbed to shore. They gathered around Finn and Lincoln, staring in awe and poking at their clothing.

"Keep your hands off the jacket!" Lincoln roared.

The children laughed and rifled through the boys' pockets, stealing Lincoln's belt and Finn's sneakers as well as Finn's and Julep's phones. They studied the device with wonder, shaking it and tapping on the glass, trying to make it work. It was obvious to Finn they had never seen technology like it before. Unfortunately, they were very careless, and he worried they might drop it into the water.

"Be careful with that!"

"What did you find, Rabbit?" a voice said. Finn watched the children part as an elderly woman stepped forward. Her face was full of wrinkles and her long hair was as gray as steel. An excited electric animal, not quite a dog or a cat, more like a fat, shimmering chipmunk, hopped around at her feet. Two glowing spheres orbited its body, producing a brilliant, crackling spark when their paths crossed.

"Spies," Rabbit said. "We found them wandering in the grasslands."

The woman stepped close, as if her eyes weren't dependable. She studied Finn up and down, then scrutinized Lincoln.

"Strange clothing," she said. "From what land do you come?

"Cold Spring," Finn said.

"There may be more of them," Rabbit said. "Proton wouldn't send just the two."

"I don't believe they work for Proton," the woman replied as she untied Finn's hands. "He's never been a friend to children, as you know. Let's start over with some introductions. My name is Anna, and these children call themselves the Runaways."

"I'm Finn."

"And you?" she asked as she untied Lincoln.

"I'm Lincoln."

"I see. Runaways! Let's give Finn and Lincoln something to eat. I suspect we are in for an interesting story, and they are usually best told over a good meal."

10

Sin Kraven was jostled awake and found himself locked inside an iron cage strapped to the side of a strange, hairy beast. Its enormous backside blasted foul gasses with every lumbering step it took. It reminded him of the bull beetles his father owned on the Plague home world, a bit like . . . What did the humans call them? Elephants? He couldn't be sure, as he had taken great pains not to learn much about Earth. His hope was that the Plague would drain the planet dry quickly and move on to somewhere less foul-smelling.

"Where am I?" he shouted as he rattled the cage door with his claws. He couldn't see who was controlling the animal, but he knew it hadn't locked him up on its own.

"Whooo-weee!" came the response. The beast stopped suddenly, and a thin elderly man with a bushy white mustache climbed down. He peered at Kraven with tiny brown eyes, spit something black onto the ground, and wiped his filthy mouth with his equally filthy sleeve. "Was that you talking, Mr. Bug?"

"Of course it was me, you old fool! I am Sin Kraven, commander of the Plague mother ship. Release me now!"

The man cheered, then danced a little jig.

"It talks! It talks! I'm rich! Say something else!"

"I will tell you one last time: let me go, or I will fry you to the bone." Kraven reached for his sonic blaster, but it was missing from its holster. "You have taken my weapon."

"Indeed I have," the old man said as he patted a bulge in his jacket. "Nice-looking shooter, too. It will fetch me a pretty penny in Quarkhaven—that is, if I don't keep it for myself."

"If you release me, I promise you an act of mercy," Kraven said.

"You hear that, Bess?" the old man said as he patted his pack animal on the rump. "It's offering me mercy. That's a rare thing in this world. Unfortunately, I'm afraid I have to decline your generosity, Mr. Bug. You see, I have plans for you and the tick-tock man."

"The tick-tock man?"

"Yeah, your friend. I found you two lying out there in the grasslands. He's in a cage on the other side of Bess. Hasn't moved a metal muscle since I laid eyes on him.

I suppose he's broken, but we'll see if we can't get him running again. Quarkhaven has a lot of tick-tock men, so we're bound to find someone who can fix him. If not, I suspect people will still pay a nickel to take a gander at you, and for a penny I might let them throw rocks at your metal friend. Folks got a lot of anger for tick-tock men, right?"

"Highbeam!" the bug growled, suddenly realizing what the old man was talking about. "Can you hear me, robot? Talk to me, you walking bucket of rust!"

There was no response.

"Found a fancy tarp, too. I'm gonna use it to make a sign: *Come See Maynard's Marvelous Circus Show!* Oh! I'm gonna be swimming in pennies," the old man said as he crawled back on top of his beast.

Kraven knew that trying to reason with this man was a waste of time. All humans were stupid, and this one seemed especially so. It was better to fall back on his soldier training and conserve his strength until he found an opportunity to escape. He settled into his cage and looked out on the vast plains that surrounded him. Everywhere humans lived was an intolerable nightmare. The only pleasure he took from that knowledge was that Finn Foley and his friends were out there somewhere, most likely suffering, too.

11

"**D**on't panic. Don't panic. Don't panic," Julep kept saying to herself, over and over, as she sprinted through the tall grass. Maybe if she said it enough times she would listen, though at that moment she had plenty of reasons to panic. A monstrous bear was chomping at her feet. At least, she thought it was a bear. It had the same shape, but it was twice the size of anything she'd ever seen at a zoo, and it seemed to be made from electricity.

It shouldn't have been that big of a surprise. Since meeting Finn Foley, she'd experienced phones from the future, alternate timelines, wormholes, talking robot heads, alien mother ships, and a subatomic slip-and-slide. If not for the bear, she would be over the moon with excitement. The old Julep, the one before the Mongoose had come along to save the world, would have been thrilled that all the things in her books were actually real.

Speaking of Finn, where was he? Where were Lincoln and the robot? When she'd woken, she'd been all alone, with nothing but her belongings and a lump on the back of her head. She'd shouted their names for an hour, which turned out to be a terrible idea since it had lured the hungry animal. She might as well have screamed "Come and eat me!" Was that what had happened to the boys? The thought sent a shudder through her. Were Finn and Lincoln inside the bear's belly? Was she dessert?

One thing was certain: she couldn't run forever. She needed a place to hide, but the only options in the endless stretch of prairie grass were a couple of shiny black hills. Wait! Wait! Was there a cave on top of one? She pointed herself in its direction, sprinting as fast as she could until she reached the base of the hill. The slope was steeper than she expected, and it wasn't going to be easy. The shininess she'd noticed before was created by flat black stones, all of which were as thin as cardboard. They shuffled beneath her feet and she instantly crashed to her knees. Ignoring the pain, she looked over her shoulder and saw that the bear was nearly on top of her, so with all the strength and speed she could muster, she dashed up the hill. It did little good. The higher she went, the more she slid. If there was any blessing, it was that the bear wasn't having any luck, either.

Exhausted, she fell to her hands and knees and crawled, inch by inch, with the enormous animal snapping and snarling less than a foot away. It felt like hours before she reached the summit, and with her last ounce of energy, she darted into the dark cave.

"Get down!" someone shouted. There was a hum and a squeal, and suddenly the darkness was alight with white-hot missiles. She cowered just in time to allow them to streak around her and slam into the bear. The creature fell backward. She could hear it sliding on the slippery stones all the way to the bottom of the hill. It howled in both agony and frustration.

A man rushed past her and out of the cave. She saw him raise his weapon, a red-hot gauntlet he wore on his hand. A streak of flame shot from the fingertips and down the slope. The bear let out another pained cry and then was silent.

"Thank you," she whispered in a shaky voice. Her hero was tall, with a ragged blond beard and a long red coat that brushed the ground as he walked.

"You can thank me by finding your own cave," he said.

"You want me to leave? What if there are more of those things out there?" Julep asked.

"I suspect there are more," he said. "Many, many more. But if you make a run for it now, there's a good chance you'll reach the hill just to the right of this one. You can camp there until the rest of the Runaways come get you."

"The who?"

"You ain't one of the Runaways?"

"I don't know what you're talking about," she said. "I'm not from here."

He stepped closer, studying her face and hands. He took off her glasses and stared into the lenses, then tugged on her shirtsleeve.

"Are there more of you?"

She nodded. "I came with my friends, but I woke up all alone. The bear showed up before I could find them."

"Did you bring anything with you?"

"Like what?"

"Weapons?"

Julep thought of her backpack, filled with sonic grenades, but decided to keep them a secret.

"No."

"C'mon," the man said, then eased himself down the rocky hill. She followed, somehow managing to stay on her feet. Once at the bottom, the stranger used his glove on the dead bear, burning off a portion of its body.

"What's this?"

"Dinner."

She helped him carry it back up the hill. He made the climb effortlessly, as if he had been doing it his entire life, but for Julep, it was no easier than the first time.

Once they were safely in the cave, the man skinned and prepared the meat, blasting it with his glove to cook it. When it was finished, he found a couple of pointy sticks and used them as skewers. He gave one to her. She sniffed at it, both curious and a little frightened. She had never eaten an animal that had tried to eat her, especially one that glowed like a lightbulb, but she was starving. The meat was sour and stringy, but her stomach was louder than her taste buds' complaints.

"Terrible, isn't it?" the man asked.

She nodded. "That's a word for it."

"I met someone like you a while back. He said he fell from the sky."

"I think I'm here to find him," she admitted, hoping he was talking about Finn's father.

"What's your business with him?"

"He's my friend's dad," Julep said. "You haven't seen a couple of boys and a really tall robot, have you?"

"Robot?"

Highbeam was too complicated to explain. She waved the man off. It was obvious he hadn't seen Finn and Lincoln.

"What do you plan to do with this man when you find him?" the stranger asked.

"Take him back home, I guess," Julep said. "There are big problems where I came from, and his son thinks he can fix them."

The stranger nodded, then finished his meal. He impaled a couple of torches in the loose ground near the cave entrance, then set them ablaze with his glove. The light allowed Julep to get a better look at his face. His eyes were small and his jaw was set and rugged. He seemed to be around her dad's age, but she couldn't be sure. His skin was wrinkled and damaged by the sun.

"Gonna offer you some advice, seeing as you aren't a local. A busy trading route runs through these grasslands. It's full of bandits, killers, and criminals on their way to Quarkhaven. It ain't safe for a kid, especially one from another world. Chances are your missing friends are headed there, most likely against their will. Either way, I got things to do that can't wait, and helping some lost kid is not one of them. You can stay the night in the cave, but in the morning we're going our separate ways."

"Understood. I won't be any trouble," she promised.

"You're already trouble." He disappeared deeper into the cave and came back with a blanket. As he was unrolling it, Julep spotted a flicker of metal in the darkness. She pushed her glasses up the bridge of her nose and saw the faint outline of a machine parked in the back of the cave. It was big and shiny and . . . Wait! It couldn't be!

"You have a hoverbike!" she said, leaping to her feet and rushing toward it to make sure her eyes weren't playing tricks on her. It was covered in dust and parked in the very back of the cave. "How did it get here? Does it work?"

"None of your business, kid," the stranger said.

"I stole one of these from the bugs a few days ago but I crashed it."

"Wait. Are you saying you can drive it?"

"Of course," she said, careful to hide her face so that he didn't see she was overselling her skills.

His eyes softened, and suddenly, she understood. The stranger had found the bike and couldn't get it running.

"I'll make you a deal. Take me to this Quarkhaven so I can find my friends, and I'll teach you how to drive the bike," she said.

"Quarkhaven is no place a kid," he warned.

"You just told me my friends might be there. I have to find them," she said. "They're my only way to get back home. Seems like a small price to pay to learn how to use a machine that flies and shoots rockets."

"Rockets?" His eyes went from her to the bike, then back.

"Rockets," she repeated, though she did not know how

to fire them. Still, if he let her drive it to Quarkhaven she'd get a chance to figure it out.

"In the morning you will drive us to my camp. It's a few miles from the city. I won't go any farther. It's the best I can offer," he said.

"Why can't you take me all the way?"

"'Cause the next time I walk through the gates of Quarkhaven, I'm bringing an army with me to burn the place to the ground."

12

The Runaways invited Finn and Lincoln to join them for dinner. The boys watched some kids lug heaping baskets of fruit to the water's edge while others built a fire to cook fish. This strange kingdom seemed to have plenty of food, and the inhabitants were generous with it, but neither Finn nor Lincoln recognized what they were given. Some of the fruit resembled peaches, but they had a ghostly glow, not unlike the walls of the cave. They also moved on their own, rolling around in the baskets and squirming in their hands.

"I can't eat this," Lincoln muttered. "It's still alive."

"Everything is alive," Anna said. "Don't worry. It's delicious and will renew your strength. You're going to need it."

Lincoln took a tentative bite while Finn watched.

Juice ran down his chin as he stared at the fruit in wonder.

"It tastes like banana bread," he said.

Finn took a bite. Lincoln was right. It was just like his mom's. He hoped it wouldn't continue to glow once it was inside his belly.

"Where do you come from, boys?" Anna asked.

Finn glanced at Lincoln. His friend used to be the fast talker of the group: as much trouble as he used to get himself into, Lincoln had charmed his way out of a lot more. But "new" Lincoln just shrugged.

"I'm not sure you would understand," Finn admitted. Now that the Runaways were sharing their dinner, he felt safe to explain what he could. "What's important is that we came here with friends—one is a girl with black hair and glasses. Her name is Julep, and she's got this really amazing smile—"

Lincoln laughed out loud. "I knew it," he said to himself.

"What?" Finn said defensively.

"You got it bad for Julep," he said.

"Shut up," Finn said, then turned back to Anna. "She might be with a robot named Highbeam. He's really tall, with—"

"A bad attitude," Lincoln interrupted.

"A robot?" Anna asked. It was obvious she didn't know the word.

"Um, yeah, like a man, but he's made out of metal," Finn explained. He stood and mimicked Highbeam's clunky walk.

"A tick-tock man," Rabbit said, her face full of concern. "You came here with a tick-tock man? I told you they were spies, Anna!"

"Is a tick-tock man a bad thing?"

"An army of tick-tock men terrorize the innocent people of this world," Anna explained. Her words came out soft and low, as if saying them louder might awaken some dangerous creature. Finn looked around at the other children. Their eyes were filled with fear. The little ones nestled against one another as if Anna were sharing a scary ghost story. "They are controlled by a man who calls himself Proton."

"With a name as corny as Proton, you better have an army of robots." Lincoln laughed.

"He's no joke. Proton seizes land, burns towns and villages, and leaves thousands homeless and hungry. Since he seized power, no one is safe—especially those that fight back," Anna said. "He takes his revenge on those that dare by hurting their children. That's why the Runaways were so rough with you. We have to stay hidden. There are many who would like to earn Proton's favor by delivering the children of his enemies."

"We don't know Proton, and Highbeam isn't one of his tick-tock men," Finn promised.

"Why are you here?" Rabbit said. She was still suspicious of the boys and wasn't hiding it.

"I was kidnapped," Lincoln muttered.

"I came to find my dad and take him home," Finn said, ignoring Lincoln's snark. "His name is Asher Foley. He may have come through here about a year and a half ago. He's tall, has green eyes. Sometimes he has a beard. Have you seen him?"

"I knew a man named Asher Foley," Anna said. Her voice sounded stiff, as if she were fighting to keep some words back.

"Can you tell us where to find him?"

"He is in Quarkhaven," Anna said.

Finn was overjoyed. There was a time not so long ago when he thought he'd never see his father again.

"That's great. All we have to do is find Julep and Highbeam and the slip-and-slide and we can get out of here," Finn said to Lincoln.

"What is a slip-and-slide?" Nico asked.

Finn did his best to explain the device to him, though he knew he sounded ridiculous. *Kid's toy, made of plastic. You spread it on the ground, get it wet, and slide on it for fun. Oh, and this one shrinks you to the subatomic level.* Anna and the kids looked at him like he'd fallen on his head.

"It would not be wise for you to go looking through the grasslands for your friends. If you are seen, you could lead others to our camp. I will send scouts after dinner. If they are out there, the Runaways will find them."

"Thank you," Finn said.

"As for Quarkhaven, it would take days to get there on foot, and there are bandits and wild animals that might harm you. Rabbit and Nico will take you on the skimmer in the morning," Anna said.

"Absolutely not!" Rabbit cried. "I'm not going back there."

Nico looked incredulous but didn't say anything.

"You know the way better than most."

"And I'm the one in the most danger if I set a foot past the wall," Rabbit said.

"This cannot be avoided," Anna said. "We cannot abandon them."

"Yes, we can!" Rabbit shouted. "They're strangers. We owe them nothing."

"We owe something to everyone," Anna scolded her companion.

"I'll be with you," Nico said to Rabbit.

His reassurance didn't seem to help. Rabbit threw down the fruit she was eating and stormed off into the darkness. The argument agitated Anna's pet. It circled her feet, shooting sparks of electricity in every direction.

"So Quarkhaven is dangerous?" Lincoln asked.

"Since Proton took control, everywhere is dangerous," Anna said. "If you've had enough to eat, would you be so kind as to help build tonight's bonfire? The lagoon can get very cold when the suns go down."

The boys wanted to earn their supper, so Finn and Lincoln followed Nico and some other Runaways toward the cave entrance. There they found a neat stack of dried sticks and branches. They collected armloads, though Lincoln complained bitterly about getting his blazer dirty. They stacked everything in the center of a stone circle near the water's edge; then Anna squeezed the juice from a prickly vegetable onto the wood. The first drops caught fire, and soon the flames were burning bright. Nico covered them with kindling until the fire was nearly five feet tall. The children gathered around the circle, enjoying the warmth and admiring the colors.

"Runaways, thank the sky for the day's blessings and for bringing us new friends," Anna called out.

A sea of blue-faced children looked up to an opening in the cave above them that revealed the subatomic sky. A dozen massive yellow moons gracefully circled one another like slow-moving dancers. Finn felt bad that his father had been trapped for so long, away from his family and his life, but at least he was in a place full of beauty and wonder.

"We ask the energy that lives in all things to look after us for another day, and we ask that it help point us toward a future where we can return to our homes and families," Anna said. "Lend us luck, and spare a little for Finn and Lincoln on their quest. Clear the roads of troublemakers and bandits, and help them find what they seek. We say this together. It is as true for one—"

"—as it is for all of us!" the children said in unison.

Everyone hugged their neighbor and wished them luck. Finn was pulled into an embrace by Nico and several others. It was kind and comforting, even though the children were strangers. When he turned to hug Lincoln, he got a hand in his face.

"Don't even think about it."

It hurt more than he let on.

The Runaways sat by the fire for hours, talking and eating and sharing stories, mostly about creatures they called electric bears, which they claimed could swallow people whole. Finn wasn't sure if they were real or just something to tease the smaller children about before bedtime. All he knew for certain was that the fire was hypnotic and warm, and with a full belly, his body was reminding him of the events of a very long day. Sleep crept up on him, and a moment later, he fell over into the sand.

"Sorry, I'm so tired," Finn said.

"I think it's time to put this day away. Nico has volunteered to host you tonight," Anna said.

Nico secured his top hat and waded into the water. The boys followed him to the structure, where they watched him scurry up one of the ladders like a squirrel. It looked so easy, but Finn and Lincoln were exhausted and awkward. Climbing to the top was humiliating for both of them. Some of the smaller children watched and giggled.

Once they reached the top, Nico waved them into one of the tiny huts. It was small but clean, with a little wooden table, a cot, and a stack of curling papers covered in charcoal drawings.

"Did you make these?" Lincoln said as he eyed them closely.

"Yes," Nico said shyly. "My mother's an artist. She taught me."

"Last summer I went to an art camp to work on three-dimensional sketches. I think it's going to look very good on my college applications."

"What is a college application?" Nico asked.

"It's a . . . Never mind."

Nico didn't press him. He took some cushions from a stack in the corner and laid them on the floor.

"Anna said all of you are here because your parents stood up to Proton," Finn said. "Is that true?"

Nico's eyes got wet and he wiped them with the palms of his hands.

"I'm sorry," Finn said.

"We should sleep. Even with the skimmer it will take all day to get to Quarkhaven," he said as he blew out his lamp.

"Nice going, loser. You made him cry," Lincoln whispered.

Finn felt the guilt in his chest. Lincoln was right. He should have kept his questions to himself, but he was just trying to understand. It didn't help that it seemed like every time he opened his mouth, Lincoln was telling him to shut it.

Frustrated, he lay down on the cushions and did his best to get comfortable. He couldn't remember a time when he'd been so tired, but his brain was on fire with curiosity. He tossed and turned, only making Lincoln more irritated.

"Will you stop?" the boy hissed.

"I wish you remembered me. A few months ago you and I camped out in my backyard. We didn't have a tent, so we used sleeping bags, but there were so many mosquitos we both wound up on my couch," he said.

"Go to sleep, Foley," Lincoln said.

"Aren't you a little interested in getting to know me? We were attached at the hip," he said.

"The other me must have been a moron," Lincoln said.

"I can prove we were best friends. Your favorite ice

cream is black raspberry soft-serve. You say it's the only flavor worth eating. How would I know that if we weren't close?"

"I don't know. You can learn a lot about other people on the internet if you're creepy enough," Lincoln said. "Leave me alone. I'm tired. In the morning we'll go find your dad and the others, and then you're taking me home immediately. Do you understand?"

Finn surrendered. He rolled onto his back and watched the bonfire lights from the beach shimmer on the hut's grass ceiling. They conjured shapes and figures that burned hot, then faded away, ever changing and never appearing twice.

13

Finn and Lincoln woke to a loud pounding. A boy with spiky red hair was in the doorway of the hut. He tossed Finn his phones, followed by his sneakers. He'd almost forgotten that the children had stolen them.

"The scouts didn't find your friends or that slip-and-slide thing. There are Brahma tracks heading toward Quarkhaven. Chances are your friends were picked up and taken there," the boy said, then dashed away without saying goodbye.

"Brahma tracks?" Finn asked.

"It's a big, stinky pack animal. Traders use them to move goods to and from the city," Nico explained. "Listen, it's first light. Time to go," he said. "We don't want to keep Rabbit waiting. She's kind of grouchy in the morning."

"And in the afternoon," Finn said.

"And all the other times," Lincoln added.

The boys got to their feet and stretched the stiffness out of their muscles. They climbed down the ladder and plopped into the water. Finn dunked himself, taking the closest thing to a bath he had experienced in a long while. The water was cold, but it woke him up. Feeling better, he crawled up onto the beach. The remains of last night's bonfire were still crackling in the stone circle.

All of the Runaways were awake, dashing around collecting food in their woven baskets. A handful of kids tossed a large net into the lagoon and waited patiently for fish to swim into it. A little girl with a freckled face gave Lincoln and Finn more of the strange fruit from the night before. Finn found he was craving it.

Anna appeared with her electric pet close behind. She smiled and told them she hoped they had slept well. Then her face went gravely serious.

"A word of warning about Quarkhaven: Do not linger there. If you attract the attention of Proton you may find yourself in his dungeon. If your father . . . if you can find him, take him away from here as quickly as you can."

Something about her expression made him nervous. She looked genuinely fearful for the boys.

"What do you think she's not telling us?" he asked

Lincoln when she went to help the children with breakfast.

"Listen, Foley. I couldn't care less. All I want is the slip-and-slide. Once we have it back, I'm out of here. You can go find your daddy without me. Understand?"

"Personally, I think going to another planet and rescuing a friend's dad would help you get into a good college," Finn teased.

"You're not funny," Lincoln said.

"The skimmer is ready," said Nico, sporting a new coat of blue paint on his cheeks. "If we want the winds to cooperate, we have to leave now."

"What is this skimmer thing you keep talking about?" Lincoln asked.

"C'mon," Nico said. "We'll show you."

Nico, Anna, and the children ushered Finn and Lincoln out of the lagoon and out through the tunnel. Once they were in the open, the group scaled an embankment and marched through a grove of tall, skinny trees. On the other side, hidden in a shallow valley, was a boat, but not like any boat Finn had ever seen. It was painted the exact same color as the high blue-green grass that spread around them for miles. Finn didn't even see it until they were a couple of yards away, which was incredible, since the boat itself was around thirty feet long with tall masts that rose about fifteen feet into the air. Four enormous wagon wheels were built into either side of the craft. Even stranger was that there wasn't a drop of water in sight.

"What is this thing?" Lincoln asked.

"It's a boat," Rabbit said defensively. She climbed up some netting on the side of the ship so she could get on board.

"Um, no it's not," Lincoln said, pointing to the wheels.

"Rabbit built it. The skimmer is easily the fastest way to get anywhere in the grasslands," Nico explained. "Quarkhaven is days away on foot, but with this we'll get there just before nightfall."

"She built this? By herself?" Finn asked. He was stunned by its size. Even if it just sat in the grass motionless forever, the skimmer was an impressive achievement, especially for a kid no older than himself. He and his dad had once tried to put together a model of the *Millennium Falcon,* but it fell apart before they could even get the seats in place.

"I'm a girl, so I'm not smart enough to build things?" Rabbit snapped. Her head was hanging over the side directly above him.

"That's not what I—"

"Don't pay any attention to him, Rabbit. He's got a lot of backward ideas," Lincoln said.

Rabbit shook her head in disgust and vanished.

Finn turned to Nico, hoping he could explain.

"It's not that she's a girl," Finn said. "It's just . . . I

mean . . . she must be a genius to build something like this. How does it work? Where's the water?"

"It doesn't need water," Rabbit shouted from above. "C'mon, the winds are getting strong."

Nico shrugged and scurried up the netting.

"I wasn't trying to insult her," Finn said.

"You do a lot of terrible things you aren't trying to do," Lincoln said.

Finn watched him climb the net.

Once they were all on board, Finn had to keep moving to get out of the way. Rabbit and Nico were like tiny tornadoes, racing here and there, tying ropes and adjusting the rigging. They raised a couple of tall sails, swung them into place, and fastened them around pegs mounted on the floor and rails. The sails caught the wind and Finn felt the boat nudge forward like a runner eager to start a race. The flapping fabric sounded like thunderclaps in his ears.

"Good luck to you!" Anna shouted from below as she and the Runaways waved to them. A skinny girl in the crowd was wearing Finn's backpack. He was tempted to ask for it back, but it didn't seem right, especially after all the generosity the children had shown them. It seemed like a small price to pay.

"Raise the anchor!" Rabbit shouted, pointing to a huge, wooden crank not far from where Finn and Lincoln stood. The boys leaped into action and together they turned the handle. Finn's muscles screamed as the skimmer's iron anchor rose link by link on its chain. Once it was off the ground, and the crank locked in place, the boat lurched forward. Finn lost his balance and fell onto the deck. The others stood their ground. They were a lot nimbler, even Lincoln, and they moved about the ship, suddenly a team, cheering and shouting as the skimmer picked up speed. Finn watched the Runaways fade into the distance.

The boat was fast, but the ride was far from smooth. It was a herky-jerky ordeal that kept Finn clinging to the railing. Lincoln, however, seemed to intuitively understand what needed to be done. Finn watched him rush from rope to rope, calling out commands and receiving them from the others. Finn tried to follow Lincoln's lead, but he quickly realized that the best thing he could do to help was to stay out of the way. This was only his second time on a boat. The first had been a ferry to a park off the coast of Manhattan called Governors Island, and its powerful motors had done the work. He remembered feeling the engines beneath his feet as the spray of water washed over his face and hair.

"How do you know what you're doing?" Finn asked when he spotted a smile on Lincoln's face. The boy was enjoying himself, despite all the hard work.

"I went to a sailing camp over in Beacon last summer," he said.

"Let me guess: College applications?"

Lincoln scowled.

"Actually, no. I just like boats and I thought it might be useful someday. You see, I think about the future."

Finn almost laughed, until he realized the boy wasn't joking. Then he felt self-conscious.

"I think about the future!"

"Really? Then tell me your plan for when we get home. You realize the bugs are going to hunt you down, right? Julep and I are going to get caught up in it. So will our families. You've ruined our lives, you know. How are you going to fix it?"

"My dad—"

"Your dad? Do you ever listen to yourself? What is your dad going to do to protect us from an alien prison?"

Finn had tried to explain his father several times to the boy, but Lincoln wasn't interested. Asher Foley could travel through time. He could go back and defeat the bugs before they ever got to Earth. He had access to super weapons and a lasso that would take him anywhere. But what was the point? It was just another story Lincoln wouldn't believe.

"What should we expect when we get to Quark-haven?" Lincoln asked Nico when he took a break from the ropes and knots.

"Trouble," he said. "More than our fair share."

14

The stink burned Kraven's antenna miles before the
city came into view. It was a foul odor of human
sweat, open sewers, and desperation. It nauseated him,
which didn't help with the effects of the endless jostling
of his cage.

Without warning, the old man stopped his beast and
scampered down from the box on top. Kraven watched
him untie a couple of blankets fastened to the side of
the animal, then hobble around to the other side, where
he couldn't be seen.

"Why have we stopped?" Kraven demanded.

"I've gotta protect my star attractions," Maynard
said when he came back around. He draped one of
the blankets over Kraven's cage. Thankfully, a couple
of moth-eaten holes allowed the commander to see

out. "Customers are gonna have to pay to get a look at you."

"I am a senior officer in the Plague High Guard," Kraven complained. "I will not be your clown."

"You're going to be what I good and well tell you to be, Mr. Bug, as long as I've got this." The old man patted Kraven's sonic blaster, hanging at his hip. He climbed back up on the animal, and with a loud "Gettup," the huge creature lumbered forward.

Hours passed, and the tiny holes in the blanket flashed glimpses of Quarkhaven. The city looked as filthy as it smelled. It was also crowded. Wagons and carts appeared alongside them, as did more animals like the one Maynard rode. Sometimes Kraven caught a face. Everyone was smeared with dirt and grime, and their eyes were hollow and hungry.

"Spoons! Perfect for eating soup and slurping milk!" someone shouted.

"I've got boxes! Imagine what you could put inside one!"

"Fine, handcrafted swords, forged from the best steels and ores!"

The sales pitches grew louder and louder with the beast's every step.

"What have you got there?" a boy shouted as he rushed to greet them. He peered into a hole in the blanket, but the old man gave him a kick that punished his curiosity.

"That's my own business," Maynard said. "Keep your eyeballs to yourself!"

"No need to be unfriendly," the boy said. "Are you looking for a guide, mister? I know all the important places and all the important people. For a penny I can make the right introductions!"

"Take me to the mayor."

"You must be a man of wealth if you want a meeting with the mayor."

"I will be," Maynard replied.

"On account of what's under those blankets?"

"Do you want to earn the penny or not?" Maynard growled.

Kraven watched the filthy boy give the old man a wide, hopeful grin. His teeth were stained and yellow. His clothes were rags. Humans were repulsive.

"Follow me," said the boy. "But you better have something good to trade at the gate. No one gets into Quarkhaven without losing something shiny."

"Don't you worry about me," Maynard said. "This isn't my first time entering the city, but it's going to be the last time as a poor, hungry scavenger. Beyond that wall is fame and fortune, boy. Now lock those lips and lead the way."

15

Julep thought that if she lived alone in a cave surrounded by electric bears, she might be up for a little conversation, but the stranger kept to himself and said nothing. Once their deal about driving the hoverbike was settled, he curled up next to the fire with his back to her and went to sleep. Julep tried to sleep, too. She used her backpack full of sonic grenades as a pillow. It was a long, uncomfortable night.

In the morning she woke to the tip of the man's boot nudging her in the ribs.

"Let's go."

Julep sat up, rubbed her eyes, and tried to shake off her body aches. Her stomach was rumbling so loud she would have happily eaten some more bear, but when she looked out of the cave, she saw that other animals had picked its body clean to the bone.

The view of the grasslands almost made up for her hunger. The morning that met her was dazzling. The subatomic was a combination of vivid natural beauty and a dash of magic. The colors were bright and creamy. Sparks fired at the top of the grass, and the sky was filled with strange, otherworldly birds, some resembling miniature dragons from a Chinese New Year parade. Yesterday she'd been too busy running from monsters to notice, but now the scenery almost brought her to tears It felt like she had woken up inside a beautiful painting.

She snatched up her pack, used her shirt to wipe the grime from her glasses, and followed the stranger as he steered the hoverbike out of the cave and down the hill, effortlessly keeping his balance. Julep tried to do the same but lost her footing nonetheless. Next came a combination of falling, tumbling, and flopping. When she reached the bottom, the stranger turned to her as if he hadn't noticed her awkward descent.

"Long ride today," he said, gesturing to the bike parked by his side.

"It would be nice if you told me where you got it."

"Found it," he admitted.

"Found it? Same place you found that flame-throwing glove?"

He nodded.

"How did they get here?"

"I don't know," he said, waving off her questions. "You said you know how to drive this thing?"

She nodded, leaving out the fact that she had only done it once and had crashed.

The stranger pointed toward a purple mountain in the distance. It was capped with snow.

"We're going in that direction," he continued.

Julep fastened her pack to a strap on the side, then climbed into the seat. She couldn't help but smile. She finally had a bike, if only for a while. Truman would not approve.

The stranger strapped his things to the side as well and climbed in behind her. He offered her a piece of jerky.

"Not bear," he promised.

She thanked him and ate it greedily as the bike rose off the ground. Once it was hovering over the tips of grass, she pointed it toward the mountain, and with a twist of the accelerators in the handlebars, she and the mystery man sped away. She glanced over her shoulder to see if he approved, but the stranger stared forward with his stony expression.

"By the way, I'm Julep," she said.

He nodded but didn't offer his name.

The wind was strong and cold, so she activated the

shields. Now they were encased in a quiet, comfortable space.

"Didn't know it did that," the stranger admitted.

"So, you're starting a war?"

"Nope," he said. "I'm ending one."

"That's a good way of putting it," Julep said. "Back home I've been trying to do the same. Problem is finding an army, right?"

"I've got an army," he said. His answers were clipped, but it was more talking than he had done since they'd met.

"And you're going to kill this Proton person? What did he do to you?"

"He took away the only thing that mattered to me."

"And what was that?" Julep asked, but again the man did not respond. "You think you're the one to stop him?"

"I think I'm the one who's going to try," he said. "Or I'll be the one who inspires others. Rebellions aren't started, they're grown."

"I get it," Julep said. "I've been trying to inspire people on my world for months. So far, my revolution is just me and my brother. We've managed to cause a lot of trouble, though. I have to believe others have been watching and waiting for the courage to do the same."

The talking stopped and the stranger offered nothing more than a few muttered directions, so Julep turned her gaze forward. They seemed to be following some faint tracks in the grass left by what she imagined to be a wagon. Her guess proved likely when they zipped past one overloaded with pots and pans and odds and ends. A monstrous creature that looked like a bloated elephant without a trunk pulled it, and an elderly couple sat on top. They seemed dumbfounded by the hoverbike and urged Julep to stop, but the stranger refused to let her.

"They can't be trusted," he said.

"They're just an old married couple," she replied. "They remind me of my grandparents in Japan."

"Are your grandparents murderous bandits? There was a time when people were what they appeared, but those days are gone. Not worth the risk."

Julep nodded. He sounded paranoid, but she didn't argue. This was his world, not hers.

The mountain grew closer and closer as the day passed. Sometimes, the stranger urged her to stop so they could scoop water from a nearby stream. The stranger shared more of his jerky, and climbed a tree to snatch some odd fruit off a branch. The flavor was hard to explain. It was sweet and tart and bitter all at the same time. She liked it enough to eat two of them and toss a couple more into the front pocket of her backpack. While she ate, she wondered and worried about Lincoln and Finn and their robot friend.

She barely knew them, but after seeing the pictures on Finn's phone she felt connected, almost like their friendship was important for the good of the world. She remembered Finn Foley as a loner, the new kid at school who seemed determined to stay a stranger. She caught him looking at her from time to time, but he was shy and awkward, and so was she, so they never found the courage to introduce themselves. It surprised her when she came across a picture on the phone of her kissing him on the cheek. She wasn't embarrassed by it—after all, it was a different her—but something about it felt . . . well, like a spoiler. It didn't seem right to know what tomorrow held. It stole the surprise, especially now, when life was so uncertain. Everything was taken from her—school, the library, friends, going to bed without the fear of monsters kicking down the door and dragging her away. She didn't want to surrender any more—even the mushy stuff. In some ways, knowing what might happen made her dislike Finn Foley. It was like he'd told her what she got for her birthday before she could open the present.

After they ate, they got back on the bike and continued the drive. A few more hours passed. They saw more wagons, and Julep was sure she spotted a couple of electric bears, but they ignored the bike. The suns sank one at a time on the horizon and the warm air turned cold, even with the shields blocking the wind.

"Go to the top of that ridge," the stranger said, pointing to a hill to the east.

Julep pointed the bike in the direction he indicated and accelerated to force it up the steep slope. Eventually, it leveled off on the crest, opening to a valley far below. What she saw shocked her to the core, and she slammed on the brakes. In the shadows near a river was a sprawling camp with thousands of tents. There were more people in it than she could count.

"What is this?" she asked.

"My army," he said. He shoved his fingers into his mouth and blasted a high-pitched whistle that echoed over the camp. The crowd below gave a wild cheer. Many danced and jumped for joy. Others pumped their fists into the air.

"That's a pretty big army," Julep said.

She steered the bike down the ridge and into the camp. It seemed as if everyone came to welcome him home at once, cheering and reaching out to touch him. Julep learned that his name was Hawkins and that he had been gone for a long time.

"When does the battle begin?" a girl shouted from the crowd.

"Tomorrow! Spread the word!" he told her. "When the first sun rises, we will take back this world!"

"Tomorrow?" Julep cried, but she was drowned out by the electrified cheers of Hawkins's people.

"Get to work!" he cried.

Julep kept the bike coasting deeper into the camp until Hawkins told her to stop. She parked at a large tent and they both got off. Two guards were posted at the entrance, and they nodded at him respectfully.

"I need privacy," he told them as he led Julep inside.

She found herself in what appeared to be a combination of a bedroom and a meeting hall. A wooden table littered with maps sat in the center. Chairs were scattered about, and a cot was nestled in a far corner. A variety of weapons—bayonets, huge hammers, chains covered in spikes, clubs, and shields—were stacked near the entrance. There was also a wooden chest with a huge padlock.

"You didn't tell me you were attacking the city tomorrow," Julep said.

Hawkins leaned over the maps and eyed them carefully.

"I don't usually share my war plans with strange children I meet in the grasslands."

"You can't do it," she said.

"And why is that?"

"My friends are there," she said.

"Then I hope they have the good sense to get out of town before I knock it all to the ground," Hawkins said.

16

"**Q**uarkhaven!" Nico called from the crow's nest. He scurried down the ladder and, along with Lincoln and Rabbit, lowered the sails. Finn stood at the bow and squinted into the suns at the mysterious city approaching in the distance. He prayed that Julep and Highbeam were there, of course, but his thoughts were on his father. What would it be like to find him? Would they move back to their old house in Garrison when they got home? Maybe he could go back to his old school and his old friends. Wouldn't it be nice if everything was the way it used to be?

Without the wind pushing it, the ship slowed to half its high speed. Rabbit steered it through a throng of wagons and bizarre vehicles pulled by hulking animals. It seemed as if the whole world was gathering outside the city's massive wooden gate, the only opening in the foreboding wall that encircled everything.

"Why are there so many people trying to get into this dump?" Lincoln asked.

"Everything important happens in Quarkhaven," Nico explained. "Selling, buying, trading . . ."

"Murder, kidnapping, betrayal," Rabbit added.

"Kidnapping?" Lincoln said as he eyed Finn. "Looks like you're going to fit right in, Foley."

"Can you see who's at the gate today?" Rabbit asked Nico.

The boy climbed up on the railing and peered toward the wall. After a moment, he turned back with a sour expression on his face.

"It looks like Baylor," he answered.

Rabbit shook her head in frustration.

"Who's Baylor?" Lincoln asked.

"He's the head gatekeeper," Nico explained. "No one goes into Quarkhaven without his approval."

"And a very big bribe. I hope you two have something to trade," Rabbit said. "Drop the anchor!"

Finn and Lincoln hurried to the crank, pulled the locking mechanism, and watched the heavy chain unfurl. A moment later, there was a loud thump. When Finn peeked over the railing, he saw the anchor half-buried in the sand. Not long after, the skimmer came to a jarring stop.

"We have to be quick about this," Rabbit warned. "The doors close at the highest moon, and the suns are already setting. If we're inside when they set, we're going to have to stay until morning, and that can't happen."

Everyone scampered down the netting on the bow of the ship and dropped easily into the dusty turf below. Rabbit didn't hesitate. She pointed herself toward the gate and rushed ahead, forcing the others to keep up. Maybe it was confidence, or maybe it was just frustration, but she pushed her way through the dense crowd, ignoring the angry looks of the people in line. Soon, the group was at the front of the mob. There, Nico pointed toward a mountain of a man with a bald head. He was wearing what looked like aviator goggles and a saggy pair of jogging pants. Sweat dripped from every pore, especially on his round, overstuffed belly. Next to him, standing on a stool, was a little girl wearing a filthy black tuxedo and a monocle in her left eye. She held a notepad and had a stubby pencil between her teeth. She took notes furiously as people entered the gates.

Finn watched how it worked. When someone wanted to enter the city, they offered the little girl a bribe. She examined each gift carefully, turning it over and over and then declaring its value. If she liked it, she passed it to her boss. If it met his approval, which almost always happened, she tossed it into a huge wooden dumpster. The offerings were all different: crude weapons, clothing, strange animals both dead and alive, baskets of food, shoes, jewels, gardening tools—they all went into the dumpster, which overflowed onto the filthy ground. Unfortunately, those who didn't have the right bribes were rejected and turned away. Some got angry. Others whined like children, begging to be let in. But when Baylor said no, he didn't change his mind. Some folks had to be dragged away by the impatient crowd.

"What do you have to give them?" Rabbit asked Finn.

Finn reached into his pocket. There wasn't much: two crumpled dollar bills, a penny, his house keys, his and Julep's phones. He would rather die than give them away. Not that they would do Baylor any good. The batteries were dead, and without a charge they were just hunks of metal, glass, and microchips, but to Finn they were priceless treasures. One had pictures of a past that he erased. The other had a future that would never be. They were his only link to his real friendships with Lincoln and Julep.

Lincoln's expression turned sour when he saw Finn's possessions.

"You're kidding me," he groaned. "No one is going to want a couple of dead phones."

"This is all I have," Finn said. "What's in *your* pockets?"

"Oh, no! Why do I have to give him something? I didn't even want to come here."

"C'mon! Julep and Highbeam could be in there."

"So what! They're strangers to me!"

"You going in or not?" the little girl in the tuxedo cried.

"Give him something, now," Rabbit muttered under her breath. "I promised Anna I'd get you into the city, but if you have nothing to offer my job here is done. Nico and I will head back to the skimmer and try to forget this ever happened."

"You would leave us here?" Finn asked.

"In a heartbeat," Rabbit said.

"Lincoln, if Julep and Highbeam are inside, there is a very good chance that the slip-and-slide is, too," Finn said. "You want to go home? That's our only hope."

Scowling, Lincoln searched his blazer pockets until he found a brass compass.

"I won this in my school's geography decathlon," Lincoln said with pride. "I was able to point out one hundred and seventy nations, as well as their capitals. I happen to hold the record at Hudson Valley Preparatory Academy."

"It's shiny," Nico said. "Baylor likes shiny."

Rabbit snatched it from Lincoln's hand before he could stop her and forced her way to the front of the line. Finn followed until they were only inches away from the enormous gatekeeper and his filthy sidekick.

Baylor was far more disgusting up close. His breath was a sour sock. He had a shrubbery of hairs poking out of his nostrils. He had seven teeth in total, and they looked like they were packing up and moving soon.

"Who's next?" the little girl asked.

"We are," Rabbit called out.

"State your business in Quarkhaven," the child demanded.

"We're looking for some people," Rabbit asked. "No more, no less."

"What do you offer as a gift? It's Baylor's birthday . . . in six months," she said. Her boss and the crowd broke into laughter.

Rabbit gave the girl Lincoln's compass. She studied it closely with her monocle, then gave it a shake. Finn watched the hand spin inside as it searched for true north. Lincoln winced as if he could feel the shaking in his body.

"What does it do?" she asked.

"It tells you which direction you are going," Lincoln explained.

"Why do I need that? I don't go anywhere," Baylor said, snatching it from his partner so he could get a better look. He eyeballed it closely. It was clear to Finn that the gatekeeper's eyesight was not good.

"It spins," Baylor said. "All it does is spin."

"It's all we have," Rabbit pleaded.

"It's not enough," Baylor said, forcing it back into her hand. "Go away."

"Boss, what about the fancy jacket?" the little girl said, pointing to Lincoln's blazer. "Hey, you! Give him the jacket."

"Absolutely not!" Lincoln cried.

"Lincoln—" Finn started.

"I already made an offering," he said. "He doesn't want the compass. It's someone else's turn. Give him your sneakers. Give him a finger! I don't care."

"He wants the jacket," Rabbit said.

Lincoln's face turned red. He crossed his arms in defiance.

"It's just a blazer," Finn said. "You can get another one when we get home."

"Oh, it's just that easy to get a blazer from the most prestigious college-prep academy in New York State?" the boy cried.

"All right, well, I guess we're stuck here, then. Such a shame, though. All those classes and activities you did to get into college were a waste of time," Finn said.

Lincoln growled. He kicked angrily at the dirt near his feet; then, in a huff, he pulled the jacket off and shoved it into the little girl's hands. He wouldn't even look at her as she inspected the fabric and the lining. She handed it to Baylor, who did the same, then slipped it on over his sweaty chest. Wet marks appeared immediately down the back and under the arms. Finn cringed. It was the absolute worst way to lose something you loved.

"Well, look at me. I'm a fancy gentleman," Baylor said, then roared with laughter. It was too small, but he didn't seem to mind. His assistant laughed as well. "Your tribute is accepted. All the wonders of Quarkhaven are yours to enjoy."

With a wave of Baylor's hand, six hulking men blocking the gate stepped aside, allowing the children to enter.

"I know you love that jacket," Finn said to Lincoln. "What you did means a lot to me."

"I hate you, Foley," Lincoln said.

The city, if that was the right word to describe it, wasn't much more than a massive flea market. There was row after row of tiny shops that went on forever. Some were poorly constructed shacks held together with tape and string, while others were nothing more than a blanket spread out on the ground. Each shop's owner did whatever they could to get a buyer's attention. They sang and did little dances, had strange animals doing tricks, and raced toward people to physically pull them over to look at their goods. Most of what they were selling was junk. One man dragged Finn by the hand to his blanket to show off a collection of doorknobs and broken umbrellas. Still, no matter what they were selling—toilet-seat lids, cracked pottery, old shoes—there were buyers haggling over the prices. There was a desperation in every sale. When a deal could not be made, the haggling often turned into a fistfight.

The most interesting thing was not the chaos, though, but the drones that zipped overhead. When arguing got too heated, the tiny bots appeared out of nowhere, barking threats of arrest. Their appearance shocked Finn. They were the first signs of advanced technology he had seen since arriving in the subatomic, aside from Rabbit's skimmer, which, though brilliant, was still made from wood and nails. The drones did not fit into the poor, simple world around him. They were super technologies, even for his world, and reminded him of some of the machines he'd seen during his trips into the far future when he had his time-traveling pajamas. Rabbit seemed both mesmerized and disgusted by them.

"Everything is different," Nico said. "They knocked down the square and the cathedral. The school is gone."

Rabbit bit her lower lip as if fighting back tears.

"All right, this is as far as we agreed to take you," Rabbit said. "I hope you find your people."

"You're ditching us?" Lincoln said.

"The deal was to get you through the gate," she said. "This is a dangerous place for Nico and me. If we're recognized, we could be killed. Plus, I don't actually like the two of you, so there's that."

"But we don't know anything about this place," Finn argued. "I don't have a clue where to start looking for my dad and my friends. You used to live here. I get that you want to go, but isn't there someone you could introduce us to? There has to be someone who can help."

"Rabbit, we can't just abandon them," said Nico. "They'll be in the palace dungeon within hours. We still have time before they shut the gates. Let's take them to see Kwami."

"That's way too dangerous," Rabbit said. "We'd make him a target if they caught us."

"If there's anyone in this city who can help them, it's him," Nico said. "And he would want to see you."

"Who are you talking about? Who's Kwami?" Finn asked.

Rabbit didn't respond. She stared at Nico for a long minute, then looked back at the gate as if she were doing some complicated math in her head. She spit on the ground, swore a little, and without another word charged down an alleyway.

"Does she just run off like that all the time?" Lincoln complained.

"That's why we call her Rabbit," Nico said. "We better keep up."

Rabbit seemed to know the city very well, though

there were times when she made a turn and had to backtrack because some landmark had been demolished and replaced with a shack. She made abrupt turns, keeping her head down the best she could, and at one point the boys lost her entirely. They wanted to call out to her, but Nico wouldn't let them. They couldn't draw any attention to themselves.

"She'll come back when she realizes we're not behind her," he promised.

While they waited, they stood by a huge tent where an old man with a wild mustache tried to lure people inside, promising an experience they would never forget. A crude sign over the tent entrance read MAYNARD'S CIRCUS OF WONDERS.

"You won't believe your eyes, people. A real-live talking creepy crawly and everyone gets a bag of rocks to throw at a tick-tock man," he promised. "Admission is only a penny."

Finn turned, curious about the tick-tock man. He was about to ask Maynard about him when Nico grabbed him by the sleeve.

"There she is! C'mon, before we lose her again."

Rabbit zipped down a quiet alleyway lined with little tin houses. None of them looked as if they had electricity or indoor plumbing, and the gutters on either side of the road were filled with all kinds of disgusting messes. A wind chime made from rusty spoons sang in a doorway. Rabbit stopped there and knocked. While they waited for an answer, both she and Nico looked up and down the street, paranoid of who might be watching.

The door of the little shack opened a crack. It was so dark inside, Finn could only make out an elderly woman's face peering back at them.

"What do you want?"

"I'm looking for Kwami," Rabbit said. "He used to live here."

"Kwami is gone. I live here now," the old woman snapped, then slammed the door in their faces.

Rabbit's face flushed with worry. She pounded on the door again.

"You're going to get me arrested," the old woman said through the door.

"I just need to know where he went," Rabbit said. "My name is Rabbit, and—"

The woman opened the door and ushered everyone inside. The space was dark and musty. Most of the windows were covered with blankets; a few were bolted shut and painted black. Finn couldn't see a thing. He heard a match strike and a tiny orange flame ignited. The old woman dipped it into an oil lamp and the room revealed itself. A small wood-burning oven sat in the center, an old mattress was on the floor nearby, odds and ends scattered about, and a dozen chubby catlike pets sparked and glowed whenever they brushed against one another. They all seemed very curious about the visitors, or they might have been hoping for food.

"You should have told me who you were first," the woman complained.

"I didn't know if I could trust you," she said. "I still don't."

"Then you're smarter than you look." The woman squinted hard at Finn and Lincoln. She ran her gnarled fingers along Finn's collar and sniffed his hair. She eyeballed Lincoln's shoes.

"More from the other place. I hope they're not as much trouble as the last one," she said.

"Are you talking about my dad?" Finn said. "Asher Foley?"

"He's looking for his dad," Rabbit explained. "I think Kwami might know where to find him."

"That is only heartache for you," she said to Finn. "Best to forget him, boy. Go back where you came from."

"Why?" Finn asked. "What do you know about my dad?"

The old woman let out a harrumph as if she was bored with the conversation, then crossed the room to a small old wooden contraption resting on a shelf. She scooped it up and put it in Rabbit's hands. It had six sides and was about as long as the palm of her hand to her fingertips.

"Kwami left this for you in case you ever came back. He said you would know what to do with it," the old woman said. "I've thought about tossing it out a hundred times. I worried it would bring me trouble. If it helps, I'm glad for you. I'm happy to be rid of it. Now go.

"Wait, we're looking for other people, too," Finn told her. "My friend Julep might be here. She's got black hair and wears glasses. And she has a robot named Highbeam. He's really tall and made of metal, like a tick-tock man, but he's not evil."

"You really should keep better track of your friends. I have not heard anything about a girl named Julep, but I may know where to find your metal man. If I tell you, you must promise to go and not come back."

Moments later they were making their way through the maze of shops. The suns had set, and darkness was consuming the city. Torches were lit in the roads to help shoppers find things.

"A circus?" Lincoln asked. "I think that old woman lied to us. Why would Highbeam be in a circus?"

"I should have gone into that tent," Finn said. "We were standing right outside. I knew something was odd about it. Look! There it is!"

They pushed their way through a crowd of people lined up for blocks to see the show. The same elderly man as before stood on a crate out front, barking about his unbelievable attractions.

"No need to push! Everyone will get to go into the tent. It's worth the wait. You've never seen anything like this before! You'll think they aren't real, but I guar-an-tee everything is bona fide! See the talking creepy crawler! Throw a rock at a real-life tick-tock man. Don't worry—he won't hurt you. He's sleeping! Then again, maybe you'll wake him up! Two pennies are all it costs for a memory you will never forget!"

"It was a penny earlier," Finn said.

Eager customers wrestled to be first. They dropped their pennies into a tin can tied to a post and went inside one at a time.

"Well, who's got eight pennies?" Rabbit asked.

"I've got one. Do you think he'll take anything else as payment?" Finn asked.

"Don't look at me. I've already given up my jacket. If you think I'm handing over my pants, you've lost your mind," Lincoln said.

"Follow me." Nico led the group around the perimeter of the tent. Finn understood his plan: he was looking for a way to sneak in, but a dozen dirty-faced kids were on the lookout. There was no way inside as long as they were on the job.

"Well, it's a tent, all right," Lincoln said. "Thanks for showing us the outside."

"You know, everything inside your head doesn't have

to come out of your mouth," Rabbit snapped. "At least he's trying."

"Don't worry. We'll get in there. You two stay put," Nico said to Lincoln and Rabbit, then turned to Finn. "You're perfect. Come with me."

"Perfect for what?" Finn said as he followed Nico into the crowd.

The boy in the top hat didn't explain. As he walked, he scanned everyone they passed, sometimes doubling back to get a better look.

"What are we doing?" Finn pressed.

"I'm trying to find the right one."

"The right what?"

"There. He'll do," Nico said, pointing to a man walking through the alley. He wore a red cape and a large, puffy hat of the same color. He had a ring on every finger and a large golden hoop in each ear, but what really set him apart from everyone else was that he was clean.

"Do you know him?" Finn asked.

"Nope," Nico said. "But you're going to pretend you do. I need you to go over and start talking to him like you've known him all your life. Be as obnoxious as you can."

"Why would I do that?"

"You ask a lot of questions. Just do it," Nico said, then darted into the crowd and disappeared.

Finn gulped and stared up at the man. The stranger stopped to smell the flowers at one of the stands. Whatever Nico wanted Finn to do seemed important, but at that moment, all Finn could imagine was the man strangling him in the street. He took a deep breath and approached.

"Hey!" Finn said. "How have you been?"

"Yes, young man. What do you want?" the stranger replied in a deep voice. He looked at Finn as if he were something foul on the bottom of his shoe. It shook Finn's confidence, but he continued.

"Um, how long has it been since I last saw you?" he said, scrambling to come up with something to say. "My mom says you've been out of town."

"I do not know you, child; nor do I know your mother," the man said with a sneer. "Do I look like I associate with vagrants? Take yourself somewhere else before I clunk you on the head."

Finn was about to walk away, fearful of a clunking, until he saw a hand creep around the man's waist. It dipped into one pocket, then the next.

Nico was behind him, pickpocketing.

"That's a terrible thing to say to your son!" Finn cried.

The man's eyes grew big, his expression alarmed.

"Listen, you little alley rat! I will call the tick-tock men if you don't vanish this instant!"

"No! You told me we would play catch; then you went out for milk and never came back!" Finn shouted. Nico's hand was nimbly exploring all the folds of the man's clothes. He needed more time, and Finn knew that causing a scene might do the trick.

"I want my daddy!" he cried.

"I am not your father."

"Why don't you love me? Why can't it be like it was? Come home! Come home to your family!"

A crowd gathered, drawn by the argument. They started to mutter angrily at the man.

"Don't be cruel to your own son," someone said.

"What kind of a man abandons his family?"

"This child is sick in the head. He's speaking non-sense!" the rich man shouted.

"You promised me a monkey for my birthday!" Finn shouted, then broke into the worst performance of his life. He pretended to sob, moaning and wailing, while Nico emptied his pockets.

The crowd got angry. They gathered around the man, shouting at him for being cruel to his son.

"How do you deny him a monkey?" someone shouted.

Finn sank into the growing mob, and soon, he lost sight of his "pretend father" entirely. Somehow, Nico had found his way back and was standing right be-side him. He held out his hand, showing eight cop-per pennies.

"The monkey was a nice touch," Nico said.

"Weren't you afraid of getting caught?" Finn asked.

Nico shrugged.

"Runaways have to learn to live by their wits if they want to survive. C'mon. Let's go find the others."

Rabbit and Lincoln were still in the line, and it had barely moved. The circus wasn't like the front gate. Finn was sure that if they tried to cut, they'd be torn limb from limb, so they waited. Lots of people lost patience and gave up, but Finn watched Maynard's kid security guards drag them back. Whatever was inside the tent was apparently worth the wait. No one had a watch, but Finn was sure two hours had passed by the time it was their turn to enter.

Nico tossed the pennies into the can and the old man handed each of the children a stone.

"What's this for?" Rabbit asked.

"Some folks are here for a little revenge . . . but you didn't hear that from me," Maynard said.

Finn and his friends stepped into the tent. A few torches lit the inside, which only made everything hot, humid, and claustrophobic. There were tapestries hung to create a maze luring the customers deeper into the tent. Each was scrawled with a different sales pitch: "You won't believe your eyes!" "Alive! On the Inside!" "See the Marvels of the World."

"This place is going to go up in flames, and we're going to be inside when it does," Lincoln said, eyeing the burning torches.

Finn ignored him and stepped forward, pushing the tapestries aside. Eventually, he rounded a corner to an open space set up like a crude theater. Sitting on a stage was a tall figure shrouded in shadows. Stones about the size of the one in Finn's hand littered the floor around him. When Finn edged closer, he noticed a bright reflection.

"Highbeam!" he cried, rushing to his friend. He knelt beside him. The rocks had done some damage. Highbeam was covered in dents and there were a few cracks on his glass face. Finn tapped on the side of his steel head. "Hey, buddy. Can you hear me?"

The robot didn't respond.

"Help me untie him," Finn begged. The knots binding Highbeam to the post were too complicated to loosen. Rabbit and Nico had experience with the skimmer, but they stood back in stunned silence. Their eyes were big and full of fear. It was clear Highbeam terrified them.

"He's not going to hurt you," Finn promised. "I told you. He's not like the tick-tock men. He's my friend."

"Move aside," Lincoln said, nudging Finn to get a better look at the knots. He went to work, slowly unwrapping them. "What's wrong with him?"

"I'm not sure," Finn said as he peered deeply into the robot's empty glass face. "When we came here on the slip-and-slide, the trip drained the battery in my phone. Maybe it did the same thing to him."

"All right, smart guy. How are we supposed to get him out of here, then?" Lincoln asked. "He weighs a ton."

"I don't know!" Finn cried. "I didn't think he would be like this when we found him. We're going to have to work together."

"Work together? He's huge, Foley," Lincoln argued.

"I will carry him for you," a voice said from the darkness. It sent icicles into Finn's veins. He knew the voice, but it wasn't possible. It just wasn't possible. He stomped into the shadows, straining his eyes, needing to prove his ears wrong, but he couldn't. Chained to the floor was Sin Kraven.

"You!" Finn cried. "How did you get here?"

The bug gestured to a tapestry hanging over its head, a familiar sheet of blue tarp—the slip-and-slide! Maynard was using it as a sign. TALK TO THE INCREDIBLE MR. BUG, it read.

Rabbit and Nico crept up behind him, their eyes even bigger than before. Lincoln joined them. He looked just as frightened.

"What is that?" Rabbit cried.

"His name is Sin Kraven."

150

Kraven let out a series of twitters and screeches Finn recognized as a chuckle.

"I am Commander Sin Kraven of the Plague High Guard. Free me and I will help you," Kraven said.

"Free you? You'll kill us!" Finn said.

"Hurry it up in there," Maynard shouted from outside the tent. "Lots of paying customers waiting for their turns."

"I am your only hope, pinkskin. Your weak and frail human body cannot lift a Nemethian Demolition Robot," Kraven said. "But I can. In exchange for my freedom I promise not to kill or harm you until we return to our world. My word is my bond."

"Your bond?" Finn said. Now it was his turn to laugh.

"Listen to me, you moronic primate! How many rocks can your robot friend take before he's destroyed? If we do not act now you will not get another chance."

"I can't trust you!"

"I hate you to the core, Finn Foley, but I need you as much as you need me. Use your tiny monkey brain! We must work together."

Finn stared up into Kraven's empty black eyes. Was a Plague soldier capable of honesty and loyalty? They weren't even loyal to one another, but the bug was right. Even if Lincoln, Nico, and Rabbit helped him, they could never drag Highbeam to safety, but Kraven couldn't be the answer. He hated Finn in both timelines. If he was free, there was nothing stopping the soldier from snapping all of their necks.

"Someone's coming," Kraven said. "Make a decision."

Before Finn could answer he heard the familiar sound of a sonic blaster's engine whining to life. When he turned, he saw Maynard standing behind him, along with a small army of children.

"Back away from the merchandise, son, or this fancy shooter is gonna burn a hole into you."

17

"**P**ut your hands in the air where I can see them," Maynard demanded as he waved Kraven's sonic blaster at Finn and his friends. The group reluctantly did as they were told. Maynard's hands were shaky, and Finn didn't want to make him so nervous he made a mistake. "What gives you the right to march into my tent and steal my exhibits?"

"They're not your exhibits," Finn said.

"I found the tick-tock man myself. He belongs to me," the old man crowed. "Them's the rules. Whoever has it owns it, and whoever wants it pays."

"Then sell him to me," Finn said.

Lincoln rolled his eyes. "With what money?"

"He ain't for sale," Maynard said.

"I am not property." Kraven pulled on the chains, desperate to free himself, but he was locked tight.

Maynard turned to his army of child security guards.

"I think they need a lesson in what happens when you steal from me. When I say the word, fall on these four and give them the beating of a lifetime."

"All right, kalari boy," Finn said to Lincoln. "Put one of your black belts to use."

"Kalari doesn't have black belts, loser!"

Lincoln rolled up his sleeves and stepped between his friends and Maynard's gang. He bowed respectfully.

"Can we settle this with words?" he asked.

"I reckon no," Maynard said.

The biggest of the bunch rushed forward only to catch Lincoln's punch to his stomach. He bent over, gasping for air, and Lincoln smashed the back of his neck with an elbow. A moment later, the kid was on the ground, unconscious. Maynard scowled and spit into the dirt while the rest of his bunch looked on in stunned silence.

"What are you waiting for? An invitation?" Maynard shouted at his gang. The children hesitated long enough for Finn to step up and clench his fists. He wasn't much of a fighter, but Lincoln couldn't take them all on at once.

"You're just going to get hurt," Lincoln said.

"Worry about yourself," he said.

Just as Lincoln sprang forward with his foot aimed at another kid's head, Rabbit snatched the torch that lit the tent and snuffed it out on the sandy ground, plunging them all into near darkness. Maynard shouted for someone to light a new one, but they were too busy taking punches to the head and belly.

Finn swung wildly, unable to see twelve inches in front of his face. He didn't connect with anyone, but there were groans and cries all around him. He heard Rabbit and Nico attacking someone, but he had no idea who it was. He only hoped they weren't fighting Lincoln.

Maynard seemed to understand that things weren't going well for him. He panicked and fired the sonic blaster, setting the tent on fire.

"I told you we were going to die in here!" Lincoln shouted. "Okay, Foley. Crazy idea: let the bug loose."

"No! I couldn't if I wanted to! I don't have a key!"

"I'll get it," Nico said.

"No!" Finn said, but everyone was ignoring him. A moment later he heard Maynard shout.

"Take your hands off me!"

The sonic blaster went off again, igniting the roof. Somehow the old man lost his grip on it, and it bounced to the ground. Another blast whizzed just under Finn's arm, burning a hole in his shirt and missing his body by a fraction of an inch. This was getting way too dangerous. He got down on his hands and knees. He had to get control over the blaster, but where was it? He reached out but couldn't find it anywhere.

And that was when bad went to worse. Finn heard the lock on Kraven's chains click open and the steel links clang to the floor. A set of enormous wings opened, and a shriek rang out over the chaos.

Finding the blaster now had a whole new purpose. Finn reached desperately in every direction, but there was nothing but sand. Even with the glow of the burning tent lighting the space, the blaster was nowhere to be seen.

"You looking for this?" Rabbit said. She was crouched next to him, the weapon in her hand. He snatched it away just in time. Kraven was hovering over him, his mandibles snapping with anger.

"Give me my weapon, boy," Kraven said.

"Not a chance," Finn said.

"You don't even know how to use it," Kraven said. "You will kill yourself."

"I'm a fast learner," Finn said.

Finn was sure the bug was going to attack, but instead he leaned down, lifted Highbeam off the ground, and hefted him onto his shoulder.

"Are you coming, pinkskin?"

"C'mon!" Lincoln shouted, rushing to Finn's side and helping him stand. He had ripped the slip-and-slide off the tent wall and shoved it under his arm. Nico and

Rabbit were urging them toward the tent entrance. Everything was on fire. Maynard and his gang raced past them, abandoning the circus, eager to save their own lives. Finn followed them out and watched as the old man snatched his can of pennies and fled into the streets.

A mob of people was gathered outside, curious about the fire. When Kraven stepped out into the light with Highbeam on his back, a cry of terror rose. Hundreds fled in a panic.

"Just a second," Nico said, taking the slip-and-slide from Lincoln and draping it over Kraven and Highbeam. It wasn't the best disguise, but it covered most of the bug's scariest parts. "Ugh. People are going to notice them."

"It won't matter. We've probably brought all of Quarkhaven down on our heads. The tick-tock men will be here any minute," Rabbit said, gesturing to the burning tent. "If we don't want to end up in the palace dungeon, we need to get out of the city before they lock the gates. Once they're shut, we're stuck here."

"I came here for my dad," Finn said. "We have to find him and Julep."

"They're going to get you killed!" Rabbit cried.

"She's right, Foley," Lincoln said. "You can come back later and look for them. Right now, the best thing to do is get out of here."

Finn scanned the group, looking for an ally, but he was all alone. Worse, they were right. The realization left a bitter taste in his mouth, but there was no other choice. He would come back by himself.

"Let's go," he said, surrendering.

"We need to move fast. We are almost out of time, and it will be a miracle if we aren't spotted," Rabbit said. She led the group through the streets while people stopped and stared.

"Hey! What's going on here?" someone shouted.

"Those kids burned down the circus!"

"People are figuring us out," Lincoln said as they ran.

"Just keep moving," Rabbit said. "The gate isn't far. We'll be safe once we're past the wall."

The heavy toll of a bell rang out. It was so loud it shook Finn's bones.

"What was that?" he cried.

"They're locking up!" Nico shouted, pointing down the alley. With the moon at its highest in the sky, a dozen muscular men pulled an enormous chain that slowly closed the massive doors to Quarkhaven. "We're not going to make it."

He was right. Even a full-on sprint wasn't going to get them through. The doors shut with a heavy thud. Finn turned to Rabbit, expecting to see an angry expression, but instead her face was painted with panic.

"This is your fault," Rabbit said as she turned to

Nico. "You should have argued with Anna. It was her against me. We are risking our lives for strangers, but she wouldn't listen."

"It was the right thing to do," he said.

"The right thing to do was to mind our own business," she said.

"Stop arguing," Finn said. "We need to come up with a plan."

"Give me my weapon. That's the only plan we need," Kraven hissed.

"Forget it," Finn said.

Rabbit reached into her pocket and took out the box the old woman had given her. She studied it closely.

"What is it?" Lincoln asked.

"A secret message," she said, sliding a panel off the front. Inside was a series of tiny wheels and levers. She spun them and the back of the box opened, revealing even more parts. She flipped it over, seemingly understanding its inner workings. Her hands moved so fast Finn couldn't keep up, but soon the object was unfolding, revealing a scroll of paper hidden in a tiny compartment. Gingerly, she removed it and unrolled the parchment.

"What is it?"

"A map," she said. "C'mon!"

Once again, they were chasing Rabbit through the alleyways and back roads. When they were far enough away from the chaos of the circus fire, the crowds thinned, and shop owners had put away their merchandise. It was clear that many of them slept in their stores and would wake up in the morning for another busy day, but some locked up and drifted into the night.

"Hurry," an old man whispered when they passed by. "You don't want to break curfew."

Rabbit picked up her pace and zipped down several more alleys until they came to a massive pile of trash nearly twenty feet high. Finn guessed it was where the entire town dumped their garbage. Rabbit searched the debris until she found a door designed to look like junk. She pushed against it and an opening appeared. Without a word, she went through it. Kraven shoved Highbeam's lifeless body through, then narrowly managed the entrance himself. Finn, Lincoln, and Nico were last. Once inside, Nico moved the secret door back into place.

Finn found himself in an enclosed street with a collection of shacks made from scrap metal. Many were nothing more than poles with roofs. The sky was completely blotted out by corrugated steel. He couldn't believe it. They were in a community hidden inside a trash heap.

Their sudden arrival caused people to peer out of shadows with alarm.

"Where are we, Rabbit?" Nico asked.

"I don't know," she muttered. "This is where Kwami told me to go."

"It stinks," Kraven grumbled.

"Shut up," Finn said. He was still holding the sonic blaster and keeping a close eye on the bug.

Rabbit took out Kwami's scroll a second time. Finn noticed that a crude map was scrawled on it, but Rabbit didn't explain. She led the group to a shack halfway up the alley and pounded on a tin door. A moment later, a scruffy-bearded man with skin and hair just like Rabbit's appeared in the doorway. He was lean and strong and looked confused.

"Rabbit?" He pulled the girl into his arms and hugged her tightly. She didn't resist at first, but after a few moments she went rigid and pulled away. "What are you doing here?"

"We need a place to stay for the night, Kwami," she said.

"Kwami? Who's Kwami? I'm Dad. Get in here," he said, peering at his neighbors as if he couldn't trust them all. One by one, Finn and the group entered his house, and the man shut the door behind them.

It was small, but there was enough room for everyone. Cushions were scattered on the floor, but there was no bed. A rusty stove sat in the corner, and there were several buckets full of water. The walls were covered with maps of the city, some with paths marked in red crayon, as if Kwami was tracing routes through Quarkhaven.

"You shouldn't have come back here," he said to Rabbit. "We risked everything to get you to safety."

"I didn't have a choice," Rabbit said. "Anna made me come."

"It's my fault," Finn said. "Your daughter is helping me find my friends and my father."

"Who's your father?"

"Asher Foley."

Kwami's face fell, but he didn't say anything.

"I went to your old house," Rabbit said. "The woman who lives there gave me the box."

"Clever, huh?" Kwami said, his voice picking up. It was obvious he was proud of his device. "I knew you would figure out how to open it."

"You're going to have to show me how you made it," she said.

"You know I will." He smiled at Rabbit so widely it looked like it hurt his face. "Give me the map."

She did as she was asked, and Finn watched him set it on fire with a match. Kwami tossed it into his stove, where it turned to ash.

"What is this place?" Nico asked.

"We call it the Sanctuary," he said, "and I'm happy to explain after you start explaining that!"

His eyes darted to Kraven, still hidden under the tarp.

The bug shook it off, revealing his enormous alien body along with Highbeam, still slung over his shoulders. He dropped the robot to the ground like he was a sack of trash, then extended his wings and gave them a shake. Finn followed his every move with the blaster, afraid to even blink. He knew from experience that Plague soldiers were fast.

"I'm not sure we can," Lincoln said. "But hang with us awhile. You'll get used to things not making sense."

Kwami didn't have a lot of food. He managed to find a couple of bruised pieces of fruit, and the children took turns taking bites. Lincoln said it only made him hungrier. All the while, Rabbit, Nico, and Finn recounted everything that happened. Kwami listened intently, as if he were committing the story to memory. He had a million questions about the slip-and-slide, the Plague mother ship, and the skimmer. When his daughter told him about her unusual boat, he beamed with pride.

"Nico, it's good to see you," Kwami said.

"Thank you. Have you heard from my family?" Nico asked.

Kwami's eyes crinkled as if he might cry.

"Nico, I'm sorry," he said.

There was a silence in the room that said everything

that needed to be said. Nico's face contorted, but somehow he managed to hold back his sorrow.

"You know who they were," Kwami continued, "and you know what they believed. Your father wasn't shy about fighting Proton, and he talked too much around the wrong people. Your mother was just as determined. We told her not to hang the flyers calling for revolution, but she said it was her responsibility to spark courage in the city. One night the tick-tock men took them both to the dungeon. The next morning, we all moved here. We knew we were next. I've done everything I can to get information about them, but I have to assume they're gone. No one comes back from the dungeon."

"How long ago was it?" Nico asked.

"It's been six months," he confessed. "I wanted to send a message, but none of the parents knew where Anna had taken you. That was part of the plan—it's safer for everyone that way. I'm so sorry, Nico."

The boy took off his top hat and turned it over and over in his hands. A storm of sadness raged on his face. He got up and hurried out of the hut, closing the door behind him.

Kwami moved to go after him, but Rabbit grabbed his arm.

"He needs to be alone," she said. "It's just how he is."

"It's not safe out there," Kwami muttered, but he surrendered to his daughter. "So many of us stood up and fought. We thought the rest of the city would join us, but they were too frightened. I can't blame them. Proton is merciless."

"Do you know my father?" Finn asked.

"Once upon a time. In fact, it was my partner and me who found him in the grasslands. Asher was sick and confused, talking nonsense, so we brought him here to Quarkhaven."

Kwami struck another match and lit a few candles. The glow bathed everyone in gold. He set some cushions on the floor and the children got as comfortable as they could; then he sat in a chair and stared at Highbeam. "Mind if I take a look at your robot while we talk?"

"You know what a robot is?" Lincoln said. "Everyone we've met calls him a tick-tock man."

"Asher taught me the word, but tick-tock men is what the people around here call them," Kwami said as he got down on the floor where Kraven had dropped Highbeam. He lifted the metallic man's head so he could get a closer look. "Though this fellow is a lot more advanced than a tick-tock man, especially after all the copies."

"Copies?" Lincoln asked.

"When we found Finn's dad, we also found some machines. Most of them were so advanced even he didn't understand how they worked, but there was one that allowed us to make copies of pretty much anything we wanted—food, clothes, machines—I thought we were going to be rich. The downside was that the copies were never as good as the originals. Some came out a total disaster. All the tick-tocks are copied from the original. What do you call your robot?"

"Highbeam," Finn said.

"Hello, Highbeam. It's nice to meet you. Normally I'd ask for permission to get a closer look, but you don't seem to hear me. If you do, then you have my apologies," Kwami said. He popped the glass face off of the bot's head, exposing a skull made of wires and circuits.

"You said you found machines with my father?"

"Yeah, strange ones, too. Back then I was a scavenger working with a man named Hawkins. We used to scour the grasslands once a week for things that fell off of caravans and wagons. When we stumbled on your dad, he was unconscious in the middle of a pile of gadgets and gizmos like we had never seen."

Finn suspected he knew exactly where those machines came from—the future. The older version of himself, Old Man Finn, bounced around time, stealing technologies to use in his war against Paradox. He must have stored them in the subatomic. Finn wondered if the old man ever suspected there were people in his tiny closet, and that what he put inside it would cause such trouble.

"Hawkins and I had to leave most of it out there.

What we couldn't carry in the wagon we shoved into a cave. Then we brought your dad back here."

"Do you think these weapons are still in this cave?" Kraven asked, not even trying to hide his interest.

"I doubt it. Hawkins was part of the rebellion. He didn't get his son out of town in time, and . . ." Kwami trailed off and was silent for a moment. "He tore out of here after the funeral. I knew where he was headed and what he intended to do. I'm sure he emptied out the cave. He said he'd make Proton pay. I hope he gets his chance."

He dug into Highbeam's head and pulled a flat black slab out of a slot. In the light of the candle he studied it.

"It's scorched," he continued. "Most of the machines we found with your father had the same problem. It's a simple fix. Rabbit, can you hand me that wire brush on my worktable?"

Rabbit grabbed the tool and sat down next to her father, leaning in to get a better look. He showed her how to clean the device, and she took over.

"She's got an eye for how things work." Kwami laughed. "It's the one thing she got from me."

"Maybe you can do something with this?" Finn said, reaching into his pocket to take out Julep's phone. It was dead, just like Highbeam. If he could get it working again, he could show Lincoln the photos that proved they were friends.

Kwami eyed it closely, flipping it over and over in his hands.

"I'll give it a try," he promised.

"Thanks. Now can you take me to my dad?"

"Finn, no—"

"I came here for him!" Finn cried,

"He's in the dungeon. I can't take you there, but I know someone who can. Rabbit's mother—"

"No," the girl said.

"Rabbit, reuniting Finn and Asher could change things in this city. Your mother can make it happen."

"She betrayed us," Rabbit said. "She betrayed everyone."

"It's not that simple," Kwami said.

"Yes it is," Rabbit snapped. "Why do you defend her? She ruined us. I had to go into hiding."

"I get why you hate her, Rabbit," he said. "I'd feel the same way if I was eleven and didn't understand how the world works."

"I understand lots of things, like loyalty and family."

"Then you should understand that there are two sides to every story," Kwami said.

Rabbit slammed the wire brush down on the floor. A moment later she was on her feet and storming outside.

"I'm going to find Nico!" she shouted.

"Humans are too emotional," Kraven said. "It's no

wonder Proton had to take control. Without him this world would be in chaos."

"He's a killer!" Kwami said.

"You say that like it's a bad thing." Kraven laughed.

"Ignore him," Finn said.

Kwami scooped up the black slab and the brush and continued where his daughter stopped. He blew on one end of the machine and slid it back into Highbeam exactly where he'd found it. Finn heard a click, then a hum and a swooshing fan noise that came from inside his friend's chest. When Kwami put the robot's glass face back on, a swarm of golden emojis buzzed across it.

"You fixed him?" Finn cried.

Suddenly, in the center of the screen Highbeam called his face, a round, rainbow-colored wheel appeared. It spun almost into a blur.

"Uh-oh. The spinning wheel of death is never a good sign," Lincoln said. "My dad's old computer did that one day and he had to buy a new one."

"We don't know if that's what it means," Finn said. "Highbeam is from another planet. Maybe a spinning wheel is a happy thing."

"Whatever." Lincoln folded the slip-and-slide into a pillow and lay on the floor. He looked as tired as Finn felt.

"We're going to have to wait and see. You two should get some sleep. I'm going to go look for my daughter and her friend. Are you going to be safe with him?" Kwami asked as he pointed to Kraven.

Finn gestured to the blaster in his hand.

"We're fine."

Kwami tossed them a couple blankets, then stepped out into the cool night air.

"Yes, Finn Foley. You should get some sleep," Kraven whispered.

"Don't be creepy or I'll shoot you."

"I'm not going to be able to sleep. I'm too wound up," Lincoln said. "I blame you."

"I know something that will knock you out," Finn said. "I'll sing 'How Sweet It Is to Be Loved by You.'"

Lincoln studied him with huge, horrified eyes.

"How do you know that song?" Lincoln said.

"Your mom used to sing it to you at bedtime. I know lots of things about you, Sidana," Finn explained.

"This 'other me' story is boring," he said. Lincoln rolled over with his back to Finn. "I'll sleep first, then I'll watch Mr. Ugly for a while."

"Among my people I am considered rather attractive," Kraven said.

Finn turned to Highbeam. He watched the color wheel spinning on his face. He hoped it was a good sign. He couldn't lose another friend.

18

Before the Plague arrived, Julep had been a proud bookworm, devouring anything she could find in the strange and bizarre section of the Cold Spring library. She loved books about witches and monsters and local legends. She wanted to understand the science behind the supernatural—ghosts, interdimensional doorways, aliens, alternate realities, black-eyed children, holes in space and time—but since she'd become the Mongoose, she hadn't cracked a book in months. Leading a two-person revolution ate up all her free time. She planned raids all day and spied on the bugs all night, working out plans with her brother, then sneaking out after her parents went to bed to cause mayhem.

It seemed like what she wanted. For months she sat on her bed, staring up at the Plague mother ship through her window, waiting for heroes to arrive and save the day. She watched the mother ship destroy the military attacks and the police. The world's armies were no match for an alien race that could travel between galaxies. It seemed like Earth was doomed. And then she heard the rumors about the boy—Finn Foley, the quiet new kid from school, who'd led an assault with the help of a robot. Mostly people talked about how the boy failed and ended up a prisoner on the ship. They complained about how stupid and reckless he had been, how his heroics made things worse for everyone. But Julep was inspired. Finn Foley was a kid, the same age as her, and somehow he had managed to get on the mother ship and cause trouble. It didn't matter that he'd failed. What mattered was that he had tried.

So the Mongoose was born. At first, she played it smart and kept out of sight, watching and waiting. She and her brother learned what time soldiers were replaced each day, and where weapons and vehicles were stored. They started to log routines, like when the bugs went out to search homes. Soon the enemy was as predictable as the sun rising every day, and beating them, or at least causing some damage to their plans, felt within reach. Her rebellion seemed glorious— noble, even—but here she was, surrounded by people who wanted the same things she wanted, and all she felt was anxiety. Hawkins and his army were planning something dangerous, something that might end up harming or even killing her new friends, and no matter how she begged, the strange man she met in the cave would not listen.

The army fed her. They gave her a blanket and a pillow and brought her a cot to help her feel comfortable. Hawkins wanted her near. It was obvious he didn't trust her. He was smart, but she was, too. When the suns were gone from the sky and night fell over the camp, she waited patiently for him to fall asleep and then went into action.

Carefully, she got to her feet, snatched her pack, then crept into the cold night air. The two guards were still outside the entrance, but they didn't stop her. In fact, they didn't acknowledge her at all. When she padded away from the tent, they didn't even watch.

She went down the path between the tents. Despite the late hour, many people were still awake, packing bags, sharpening weapons, and preparing for the next day's fight. She could hear how eagerly they talked about their plans to wipe Quarkhaven off the map and bring Proton to his knees. The more the fighters talked about his crimes, the angrier they got. It had been the same at dinner. She couldn't blame any of them. It almost seemed as if every person in the camp had been personally victimized by Proton.

Eventually, Julep made her way to the back of the

camp, where they parked the hoverbike. Someone at dinner had mentioned that Quarkhaven was five miles away. She'd never make it on foot, not out in the cold in a world full of electric bears. It didn't feel right to take something that might help these people win their war, but she needed the bike. She only hoped she could get to Quarkhaven fast enough to find her friends and get them to safety. She strapped her backpack to her seat, climbed on board, and scanned the control panel between her legs. She was just about to press the power button, when she realized she was not alone.

"That wouldn't be your best idea," Hawkins said. His metal glove was glowing an angry bright red.

"I have to get my friends out of the city before you attack," she said.

"And you were going to steal my bike?"

"I was going to borrow it."

His eyes were hard. Pressing the power button and blasting off was an option, but she worried she might not be able to outrun whatever came out of his glove.

"I need it," she begged. "Please! You have to understand. The people I came here with are innocent."

"Get off my bike," he said. He snatched her pack and hung it off his shoulder. She stared at his glove. She could feel its heat rippling against her bare arm. "I want to show you something."

When she resisted, Hawkins grabbed her by the arm and dragged her back into the camp, down a narrow path between tents.

"This tent belongs to Harley and Dusty," he said. "They're twin brothers who used to own a small farm near Carterville with their mother. Proton and his tick-tock men stomped through it and burned it to the ground. They killed the twins' mother for no reason. She didn't put up a fight.

"This one belongs to Vida and her daughters, Tulia and Sienna. Her husband worked at a shop in Quarkhaven. He sold pots and pans. Proton had him killed for looking him in the eyes."

They kept walking down the path, passing tent after tent.

"This one belongs to Jiminy. He lost his hand when the tick-tock men attacked the town. And this one is Diana's. She hasn't seen her son Justin since he was arrested a year ago. Here's Breanna's tent. She's blind in one eye because one of Proton's guards backhanded her into a wall. Over there is Shianne, who hasn't said a word since his wife was killed in front of him. This is my army, a collection of innocent people who do not deserve to be caught in a war. Chances are that they will all be killed tomorrow, and they all know it, but they are going to fight nonetheless. Proton marched into their homes and took everything from them. They have nowhere else to go, so they have decided to fight. And you want to steal from them?"

Julep couldn't help but see the suffering. What had seemed to her like a group of lunatics, maybe even a cult that worshipped Hawkins, now came into focus. These were desperate people with nothing left to lose. They were the ones willing to fight when everyone else was a coward, but their troubles didn't change anything. Finn, Lincoln, and Highbeam were still inside Quarkhaven, and she couldn't let them get hurt.

"You're worried about your friends," he said, seemingly reading her mind. "I understand. All these people are my friends, and I'm worried about them, too, but Proton has to pay."

"There's a difference. These people know what they're getting into," Julep said. "Finn and the others don't have a clue. They deserve a chance to get to safety while they still can. It's not right to put them in the middle of your fight."

"Everyone is in the middle of this fight. The problem with your plan, girl, is that you will get caught, and a kid with a . . . what do you call it? A hoverbike? That's going to tip Proton off to what we're doing out here."

"So I'm supposed to let them die?"

Hawkins stared at her for a long moment, then waved for her to follow. He made his way down the aisle to his tent. Once inside, he knelt beside the wooden chest, took a key from his pocket, and unfastened the lock. When he opened the lid, Julep was stunned to find a set of wooden stairs leading into a dark hole.

"What is this?" she asked.

"A secret," he explained as he climbed into the trunk. He reached for her hand. Reluctantly she gave it to him and the two descended into the darkness. "Most of my people don't know this exists, only the ones who helped me dig it. I needed a place to hide some things."

He used his glove to light a torch at the bottom of the steps, and proceeded down a long, lonely tunnel. At the end was a stack of strange machines as tall as Julep. She eyed a few, baffled by what they were and what they did.

"These aren't from here, are they? Just like the hoverbike?" she asked.

"I found them when I found Asher Foley."

"My friend's dad."

Hawkins's eyes grew. Julep didn't understand why, but something she said surprised the man. His face went dark, and something in his expression told her he was struggling with a war inside his own head.

"That can't be true," he muttered to himself. "If you . . . you could hurt him. You could get some justice."

"I don't understand what you're talking about," she said. "Who hurt you? Asher?"

"Proton hurt me, but no! He's not going to turn me into a monster," Hawkins said.

Julep still didn't understand what he meant, but she was afraid to press him for more information.

He shook off his anger and his expression softened. When he was calm again, he reached into the pile of weapons and pulled out a case. He flipped open its latches and Julep saw what looked like a harness with a black helmet attached. "You can't have the bike, but you can have this. Maybe it will help you find your friends and get them to safety."

"What does it do?"

"It turns you into a bird," he replied.

"Huh?"

"C'mon. You don't have a lot of time," he said. He led her back through the tunnel, up the stairs, and out of the chest. He locked it behind them, then marched her out of the tent.

"Where are we going?" Julep asked, but Hawkins waved her off. He kept walking until they were out of the camp. When they were a couple of hundred yards away, he turned and placed the case in her hands.

She opened the case and removed the harness. A hard shell slipped over her shoulders, almost like what an umpire might wear in a baseball game. Hanging from cables at her shoulders were two handles with red buttons on top. Hawkins slipped it over her head and it automatically adjusted itself to fit snugly on her frame. Then she put the black helmet on her head. The windshield lowered on its own and the visor came alive, pumping out maps and numbers and streaming data right before her eyes. It said something in a language she didn't understand, but she got the sense it was asking her if she was ready to go.

"I think it works with your brain—at least for navigating—and it doesn't seem to run out of fuel, either. There are buttons for up and down. That's really all I know. It's yours. I hope it helps."

"Why are you giving me this? Won't you need it?"

"I'm not so great with heights," he admitted.

It was an amazing machine, more than she could ever have hoped to have. Giving it to her was incredibly generous, and she felt a pang of guilt for trying to steal the bike. These people needed every weapon and tool they could get their hands on, so she took her backpack from him, unzipped it, and reached inside.

"What's this?" Hawkins asked as he stacked half of her sonic grenades in his hands.

"Push this red button, let the clock count to three, then throw it. The explosion will be powerful, so, you know, be careful," she said.

"Thank you."

"Rebels have to stick together, right?" She slipped her backpack over her shoulder.

Hawkins pointed at a constellation in the eastern sky before he spoke again.

"Follow those stars. They'll lead you to Quarkhaven. We will be leaving soon, on foot, and won't arrive until daybreak. You have until then to find your friends and get away from the city. I can't give you any more time."

"I'll make the most of it," she promised.

Moments later, Hawkins disappeared into his camp with his armful of grenades.

The back of the harness whizzed and hummed. It seemed almost eager to show off. The helmet continued its chatter, and the visor highlighted the button in her right hand. She hoped it was giving her instructions. Taking a chance, she pressed the button, and with a blast of energy, she rocketed into the sky, screaming all the way. In the visor she saw an outline of a human body. A red flashing light blinked where the heart was located. She guessed that it was supposed to represent her. The helmet was worried about her having a heart attack.

"Okay, I get it. I need to calm down," she said, even though she was still shooting upward with no sign of stopping. She took several deep breaths and let them out slowly. It made her feel a little better, and the red warning light dimmed. When she looked down, she could see that the button near her left hand was now glowing. She pushed it, and instead of going up, she flew toward the horizon. A map appeared on the screen, and when she focused on a specific direction with her eyes, the suit changed her trajectory. With a little practice, she pointed herself north, toward the constellation, and hopefully toward Quarkhaven.

Julep was terrified of falling, or pressing the wrong button and causing a nosedive, but being able to soar above the ground felt like being inside a pop bottle. It was exhilarating. She felt full of power, like she did when she wore the Mongoose's mask. She wished she had it right then. Oh! Truman would flip out if he knew what she was doing. He'd probably scold her for fooling around, but he would be jealous. His sister was like one of his drones! She crossed her fingers that she'd find her way home and show him herself.

Something flashed and the voice returned. Words in a bizarre language slid across the visor. They all looked like hieroglyphs to her, but they were clearly asking her something.

"I don't understand."

A map of the terrain appeared on the screen. It wasn't just a collection of dots and locations. It was topographical, or rather, it showed where mountains stood and the height of their peaks. There was a way to tell the depths of valleys and how wide a river was—all displayed in three dimensions. She wondered if the helmet was asking her for a destination.

"Um, I want to go to Quarkhaven," she said.

There was a *ding,* as if the helmet was rewarding her for cooperating, and then a bright blue dot appeared on the map. She felt the suit change course and make a straight path to the town.

"I love this thing!" she cried.

The helmet chirped again. The blue dot grew, and soon she could see the lights of a town and what looked like a wall surrounding it. As she got closer, she could make out buildings. But it was the stink of the place that grabbed her attention. It reeked, even from miles away. This was the center of the world? It was in desperate need of a mop.

The visor brought up a map of the city for her, showing her streets and alleys. Quarkhaven was laid out like a big square and each corner had its own lookout tower. They glowed red on the screen as if they posed danger, so without prompting, the rockets sent her higher and higher into the sky. From up there, she could see an enormous building on the far side of town. It had huge columns and a glistening gold-and-glass dome. It was a palace, a shocking contradiction to the town that surrounded it. She guessed it was where that jerk Proton lived. From what she had heard of him, he seemed like just the kind of person who would flaunt his wealth and power in the face of such terrible poverty.

She sailed over the wall, and without warning, the rockets on the harness died. She fell from the sky, plummeting faster and faster, with the wind stealing her screams. She pressed the button by her right hand, then the button by her left, but nothing happened.

"Hello?" she cried. "Help!"

Why had she trusted Hawkins? He'd dumped a defective machine on her. She was a fool! And worse, she was going to be a dead fool. She braced for the crash, sad that her brother and parents would never know what happened to her. Sad that she couldn't warn Finn and Lincoln about the war.

However, when she was mere feet from the ground, she felt the pack roar back to life, fighting gravity to keep her from splatting. It was jarring, but she let out a joyful cheer. And then she was gently lowered, inch by inch, until her toes touched the ground. Once she had fully landed, the machine and visor powered down. There was a little chirp, as if it was saying goodbye to her, and the visor went dark.

She pulled off the helmet and took a few deep breaths to calm her shaking hands. Quarkhaven was as filthy up close as it was from the sky. The streets were lined with little shacks made from scrap metal.

A few had hints of burning candles in their open windows, but most were dark. Her arrival didn't attract any attention. She was surprised. The machine wasn't exactly quiet.

"All right, Julep. You're here," she said. "Now where are those knuckleheads?"

Finding Finn and the others was the murky part of her plan. First, she didn't actually know if they were in Quarkhaven, and second, she had no idea where they might be if they were here. There was a third problem—how she'd get them out even if she did find them—but she pushed it aside. One step at a time.

Before she had a chance to solve anything, she was engulfed in a blinding light. When she looked up, she realized she was standing in the center of a spotlight coming from one of the town's four towers.

"Mongoose! Getting caught by a watchtower is a rookie mistake," she scolded herself. "Truman would be furious!"

A loud thump rocked her ears. It was followed by another. They were accompanied by the sounds of grinding metal and gears. It was a very familiar noise.

"Highbeam!" she cried. "Is that you?"

But it wasn't Highbeam. From around the corner came a massive machine, like a jeep with legs and arms. It was painted silver and black and had what appeared to be cannons mounted on either side. A light shone from one of the windows and scanned every surface of the road until it landed on her.

"HALT! YOU ARE IN VIOLATION OF CURFEW!" a voice boomed. "DROP TO YOUR KNEES AND SURRENDER OR YOU WILL DIE."

19

It was late when Kwami shook him awake. Finn was confused, like he was underwater. It felt as if he was coming back from the dead. He shook his head to knock loose some of the sleep and suddenly realized what he had done.

"Kraven!"

"It's fine," Kwami whispered, pointing toward the sleeping monster. Kraven was exactly where he'd been the last time Finn had seen him. "He was tired, too. I've kept an eye on him."

He bent over and handed Finn the sonic blaster.

"Thanks," Finn said.

Kwami lay down next to his daughter. He watched her while she slept, then closed his eyes. Soon, he was asleep, too. It made Finn ache for his own dad.

"What is your goal in all this?" Kraven said, suddenly awake.

"My goal?"

"Why did you come to this place?"

"I told you. I'm trying to find my father," he said.

"Humans are very attached to their parents," Kraven said, as if it was an insult.

"And Plague aren't?"

"I was one of fifteen hundred hoppers," he said. "And I was expected to kill my siblings if I wanted to survive. Your face says you find that troubling. Life on my world is brutal and unkind. Only the strong live to see tomorrow. To grow to adulthood tells others that you are a formidable enemy."

"You sound as if you're proud of all that killing," Finn said.

"I suppose you could say I am," he said. "My father was not a great locust. He held no rank in the armada. He owned a farm. He made a decent amount of money and paid his tributes to the empire on time. It was my achievements that brought him glory he could never have attained on his own."

"Do you miss him?" Finn asked.

"I barely knew him," Kraven admitted. "How did your father find his way to this place?"

"I sent him," Finn said. He couldn't think of a way the bug could use the information about Old Man Finn against him, so he decided to talk. "Or at least, a future version of myself did."

"I do not understand."

"I had a time machine and I used it to kill a monster called Paradox that wanted to unravel the universe and force my father to watch. I hid my dad here, in the subatomic, where Paradox would never find him. Unfortunately, he didn't have a way get back on his own."

"Your people possess the ability to travel through time?" Kraven said. Despite his hard, motionless exoskeleton, Finn saw a bit of alarm in the bug's face.

"No," Finn said, though he considered lying just to increase Kraven's fear. "But my father does, and when I bring him home, he's going to make everything right again, just like it was always meant to be."

"Explain, human."

"It's my fault the Plague conquered Earth. I changed the past, and there were consequences. The first time, I beat you. My friends and I kicked your butts all the way across the universe."

"You're lying," Kraven said.

"You know I'm not," Finn said. "I had a lunchbox that opens tunnels through space. I had a time machine made out of pajamas. Now I have a slip-and-slide that sends me to the subatomic world. It seems anything is possible these days."

Kraven studied Finn's face for a long time. Maybe he was looking for hints of a bluff. When he didn't see any, he growled and spit something black onto the floor.

"Boy, I have been to over a hundred worlds since I joined the armada. I have looked into the faces of a thousand different species. All of them thought they were unique, and special, and destined for something great. They all believed they could save their worlds, and they put their faith in their big plans and whatever weapons they had on hand, but all those worlds fell, and all those people died, and my people consumed everything they had to offer. Earth will be no different from the others. You are fooling yourself if you think otherwise."

Finn shuddered at the thought, but it just made him angry.

"You're surrounded by smaller, weaker people, so you think you can't lose, but just like every bully I've ever met, it only takes one lucky punch to put you on your butt."

"And that is why people like you will always surrender to my kind. You depend on luck, and it lets you down every time," Kraven replied.

BOOM! The little house shook. A pot fell off a table and clanged to the floor. Everyone woke with a start.

"What was that?" Lincoln asked. He sat up, startled and groggy.

"Dad?" Rabbit shook him awake.

Nico went to stand, but Kwami stopped him.

"Stay here! It's just a tick-tock man. They patrol the city day and night. It will probably pass, but be prepared to run." Kwami sprang from his cushions and threw open the door. In a flash he vanished into the alley, joining a small group of people already gathered.

BOOM!

Someone screamed. There was a terrible crashing sound not far away, and a flood of people ran past Kwami's house.

Kwami raced back inside and pulled up a rug. Underneath were some loose floorboards that hid a long object rolled in fabric. When he unwrapped it, he revealed what looked like a walking cane about three feet long. He slammed one end of it on the floor and Finn watched it quadruple in size until it was taller than Kwami. Finn had never seen anything like it, but he was positive it came from the future.

"A gift from your father," Kwami explained.

Finn heard a buzzing that sent Rabbit and Nico into the street. Kwami followed, begging them to go back inside, but they refused. Curious, Finn craned his neck out the doorway, doing his best to keep one eye on Kraven. The noise was coming from overhead, but the steel roof over the street prevented him from seeing what was causing it.

"Sounds like one of those drones," Lincoln said.

Finn nodded. "Maybe."

Suddenly, the front entrance to the secret alley crumbled. A robot as big as a truck smashed through it and charged in their direction. It was nearly ten feet tall and had two rocket launchers mounted on either leg.

"VIOLATION! YOU HAVE BROKEN CURFEW! DO NOT MOVE OR YOU WILL BE FIRED UPON," the robot demanded. Finn knew this was one of the dreaded tick-tock men he had heard so much about. It was a hulking monster of steel and wires. Worse, it wasn't alone. Four more followed, wreaking havoc with every step. Their attention seemed to be focused on something flying over the secret community. Finn was sure the machines were chasing it and had accidentally stumbled upon the Sanctuary.

"NUMBER FOUR, NUMBER TWO, CONTINUE PURSUIT. NUMBER EIGHT, NUMBER NINE, ASSIST IN DESTROYING THIS ILLEGAL SETTLE-MENT," the lead tick-tock man commanded. Two of them followed instructions and leaped through the ceiling, knocking a monstrous hole in it, while the other two threw punches that demolished the shacks in the alley. "SUBMIT YOURSELF TO ARREST."

People came out into the streets in a flood. Finn was stunned by how many there were and angry that these lifeless machines were demolishing their homes. Some of the people fought back, throwing bricks and rocks, but they bounced off the robots. Others seemed to understand that fighting was pointless. They ran to the opposite end of the alley as a tick-tock man fired rockets in their direction. If Lincoln hadn't knocked him to the ground, one would have hit Finn right in the chest. The boys watched it explode in a ball of fire and smoke.

"You saved my life," Finn said.

Lincoln helped Finn stand and they pressed their backs against a house to avoid being trampled by the panicked residents.

"Well, I can't let you die," Lincoln said.

"It was the song, wasn't it? Want me to sing it to you again?"

"Try it and I'll kill you myself," Lincoln cried.

"Do you see Kraven?" Finn asked.

"There!" Lincoln shouted. He pointed down the road to where the bug was caught in the crowd's tide. Highbeam was on his shoulder. It was bewildering. Kraven was keeping his promise.

"Hey, dummies!" Rabbit said as she, Nico, and Kwami rushed to their sides. "You really don't want to hang around here."

They sprinted away from the approaching robots.

Finn and Lincoln followed close behind, until Finn realized they had forgotten something important.

"The slip-and-slide!" he cried.

"Leave it," Nico begged.

"There's no way to get home without it," Lincoln said. "C'mon!"

The boys split off from the others and turned back toward Kwami's house, fighting against a stampede of terrified people. They begged for the crowd to let them pass, but no one listened. They both got knocked down, but each time the other stopped to help. After collecting a lot of bruises, they reached Kwami's shack. A tick-tock man was next door, kicking the house down with one of its enormous feet.

"We have to make this fast," Lincoln said as he shoved Finn into the little house.

"You should have stayed with the others!" Finn cried.

"You think I don't know that?" Lincoln shouted. "Where is it?"

"I don't know. Look everywhere!"

The boys tore the place apart in their desperate search. Outside, in the alley, they heard the boom of the robot's foot as it stomped closer to Kwami's house.

"It's not here!" Lincoln cried.

"It has to be! It didn't just sprout legs and walk away," Finn said.

"Actually, maybe it did," Lincoln said.

"Kraven!"

Before they could race off to catch the bug, Kwami's roof peeled away and was tossed aside. Finn looked up and saw a tick-tock man staring down at them like they were a couple of hamsters in a cage.

"SUBMIT TO ARREST."

"Hard pass," Lincoln said. He grabbed Finn by the collar and dragged him into the alley. They hadn't taken more than a couple of steps when they heard Kwami's house crash to the ground behind them. They didn't look back to check, not even when they heard the robot's heavy feet stomp in their direction.

"I knew we couldn't trust him," Finn said.

"Get mad about it later," Lincoln said. "Optimus Prime is trying to kill us."

There was another heavy thud of the robot's feet. It was closer than the last.

"It's faster than us," Finn cried.

"Maybe I can help," a voice said from above.

Finn barely had time to look up before he and Lincoln were yanked off the ground, not by the robot, but by a person. With their feet dangling, they soared higher and higher, through a hole in the roof of the Sanctuary. He wasn't proud of himself, but Finn screamed in terror. So did Lincoln.

"Calm down," the flying person shouted over a loud buzz. "It's me! Julep! Saving your lives! I'm getting you out of here."

"Where have you been?" Lincoln cried.

"Well, there was an electric bear, then a hoverbike, and I was invited to join an army. I got here as soon as I could," she said.

"We'll catch up later. Kraven has the slip-and-slide," Finn shouted.

"Who?"

"The bug that tried to kill us on the mother ship," Lincoln said. "And he's got Highbeam, too."

"Hang on. My helmet is talking to me," Julep said. "Oh, I think I've found our bug."

Without warning, Julep soared higher, taking the boys along for the ride.

"Not higher!" Finn cried.

"I have to get a better look from up here," she explained. "Trust me. I'd love to set you down. You guys are heavy."

Finn watched the ground get farther away. He worried Julep was going to drop him. He and Lincoln locked eyes. They were sharing the same fear. It didn't help that the tick-tock men were firing rockets in their direction. One zipped past, missing them by inches and forcing Julep to fly through its trail of smoke. She zigzagged, avoiding a second rocket, then a third.

"I found him!" Julep said, seemingly unfazed by the attack. "Okay, we're going down. Don't panic."

"Why would we panic?" Lincoln asked.

The trio dipped fast and the boys screamed all the way down. When they were a few feet off the ground, Julep did her best to pull up. Unfortunately, the extra weight of the boys was too much and they all slammed into the street. Kwami, Nico, and Rabbit were nearby to help them to their feet.

"Can we walk the rest of the way?" Finn groaned.

"We need to run," Kwami said.

Despite the aches and pains, Finn tore off down the road in the pitch darkness of night, following the rest of the group. The other inhabitants of the alley broke off, hoping to lose the robots, and soon it was just Finn and his friends.

"Where are we going?" Rabbit said.

"We have to find Kraven," Finn said. "He's got the slip-and-slide and Highbeam."

"I spotted him heading north," Julep said.

"Fine. Where's Nico?"

Finn scanned their surroundings. The boy in the top hat was missing. How did they lose him? Finn was sure Nico had been right behind him just a moment ago.

Kwami rushed back the way they came. When he

got to the corner, he looked down the cross street and threw up his hands.

"Nico! No!"

Finn and the others ran to his side. There they saw Nico standing in the street, swinging a rock in his sling as a tick-tock man approached.

"YOU MUST SUBMIT TO ARREST!"

"Nico, run!" Kwami said.

"These things killed my family. I should have been here. I could have saved them," the boy said.

"That's not true," Rabbit said. "You would have been killed, too. Stop this right now. We can escape."

Nico didn't answer her. He just kept swinging his stone faster and faster.

"DROP YOUR WEAPON!"

Kwami slammed the tiny cane he was carrying onto the ground, and like before, it tripled in size and glowed bright green. When the first of the three tick-tock men was close enough, he swung it with all his might. Finn watched the robot's enormous leg vaporize. The monstrous creature toppled to its side as Kwami nimbly leaped to safety. When he landed, he swung his weapon again, this time against the robot's head, and like the leg, it turned to dust.

The other two robots came around the corner, trampling their fallen partner as if he were an old newspaper lying in the street. One caught Kwami off guard and snatched him in its huge iron fist. Rabbit's father cried out in pain and dropped his staff to the ground.

"Put him down!" Rabbit shouted. She was no match for the metal monster, but she sprinted forward nonetheless. With its free hand, the tick-tock man swatted at her, but Rabbit leaped out of danger.

All the while, Nico swung his sling and stone, refusing to back down.

"You killed my parents," he shouted, then let his stone fly right at the tick-tock man's face. The rock smashed its eye. As the robot shook its head, seemingly confused by the loss of vision, Niko reloaded his sling.

"THIS IS YOUR LAST CHANCE. SURRENDER NOW OR CAPTURE TECHNIQUES WILL ESCALATE," one of the robots said.

"What does that mean?" Julep shouted.

"I think it's saying it's tired of being Mr. Nice Guy," Lincoln shouted.

"Fine. I'm tired of it, too." Julep reached into her backpack and pulled out one of her sonic grenades. She pressed the button and without hesitation heaved it at the robot closest to her. The explosion was incredible. The machine flew off its feet in a blast of fire and smoke. The crash was so intense it felt like an earthquake. When the smoke cleared, the tick-tock man was a mess of wires and melting steel.

"You don't happen to have another one of those, do you?" Finn cried as he pointed to the last robot.

"Sure," she said, reaching into her pack and tossing him a second grenade. Finn wound up, ready to heave it at the last tick-tock man, but just before he could throw it, the robot grabbed Rabbit and lifted her off the ground. If Finn tossed the weapon, it would kill her for certain.

Nico charged forward, whipping his sling and stone. "Nico! No!" Rabbit shouted.

The boy didn't listen. He fired one stone after another, desperately trying to stop the robots, but most of his rocks pinged off their metal skin without doing any damage. It didn't matter. Nico didn't back down. His face was pain and loss. Tears poured down his cheek. He was all fury and heartbreak.

"Fall down!" he shouted as he sent another stone flying. "Why won't you fall down?"

The robot threw a punch. It hit the boy with a shocking impact. Nico's body snapped backward and went sailing into a wall. He collapsed to the ground like a broken doll. His top hat fell into the dusty street.

"No!" Rabbit screamed.

The eyes of the remaining tick-tock men glowed red, and strands of electricity danced along their torsos and into their arms. Rabbit cried out as the energy seized her body. Kwami did the same. Both lost consciousness, and the robots dropped them into the dirt. Before they could react, Lincoln and Julep were yanked off the ground and electrified as well.

Finn was alone in the street, all his friends hurt or dead, as the robots turned their attention to him.

20

Getting out of the alley was impossible. The mob nearly trampled Kraven to death. Luckily, he found a deserted shack to hide in. Once inside, he tossed Highbeam onto the dirt floor and peered through the window. People were still fleeing, though a few fools were trying to fight the tick-tock men. What a waste of time. The machines were enormous and destructive. He admired the fear they created. It was inspiring. When he got back to the mother ship, he would build the Plague a version of their own. Having an army of tick-tock men would save time and effort with troops on the ground. He would surely be honored for his vision. He'd be the youngest admiral in armada history.

Fortunately, the tarp that had brought him to the subatomic world was now in his grasp. What did the boy call it? A slip-and-slide? The foolish child had gotten so excited by the robots that he'd run into the street to gawk at the attack and left it behind. It was a foolish mistake. Kraven regretted that he wouldn't get to kill Finn Foley, but stranding him on this primitive trash planet was a suitable revenge.

He tossed the shack owner's meager belongings aside and unrolled the tarp on the floor. There was just enough room to run and leap onto it, like he had done the first time, but how did it work? There were no controls to make him bigger. What if he dove onto it and it made him even smaller? He couldn't know, but he would have to take the risk, and fast. One of the tick-tock men would find him soon enough.

He scooped up Highbeam once again, grunting at the machine's bulk and weight. He would be useful once the proper head was attached to his body.

"Take me to the mother ship," he said out loud, hoping the slide worked on voice commands, and with a burst of speed and a mighty leap, he dove headfirst onto the plastic. He crashed hard, tumbling end over end, until he slammed into the wall. The impact nearly knocked the house over. Dazed and in quite a bit of pain, he staggered to his feet. Why was he still in the subatomic? What did he do wrong? There was hardly anything to it the first time he'd used it. Why wasn't it working now? Maybe he'd run at it from the wrong end. Securing Highbeam again, he took a deep breath and leaped headlong onto the ground. Once again, he crashed hard and knocked the wind out of himself. He rolled into a chair and broke it to pieces.

"This makes no sense!" he growled. "When I get back, I will kill Pre'at. I don't care how valuable she is to the armada. Robot! What am I doing wrong?"

Highbeam said nothing. The only sign of life was the swirling disc of colors on his faceplate.

Outside, people were still screaming and running. Kraven felt the ground shake from one of the robots' heavy feet. It was close, too close. Kraven was running out of time. Desperate, he bent over and flipped the tarp onto its other side. Maybe it was as simple as that. Preparing himself again, he put his head down, darted forward, and leaped, with the same painful results.

"Finn Foley!" he yelled, knowing that his failure was somehow the boy's fault. The pinkskin knew something he didn't. Once again, his own arrogance was his un-doing. He should have dragged the boy with him, but now? There was a good possibility that the human was either dead in the street or captured. Frustrated, he snatched the tarp and rolled it back up, then huddled in the shadows, waiting for the machines to do their destructive work. He only hoped Foley was still alive, or the great Sin Kraven was going to die on this stinky, worthless planet.

21

Finn woke up in a huge marble-floored room with ivory columns holding up the ceiling. His body felt achy, and there was a metallic taste in his mouth. The tick-tock man had warned him not to move. Finn should have listened.

"Where are we?" Lincoln asked. Finn turned to find his friends waking up nearby. Julep and Rabbit and her father were there, too. Finn bit his lip to keep from crying when he realized Nico was nowhere to be seen.

"We're inside the palace," Kwami said. He sounded worried.

"They took my jet pack and my grenades," Julep complained.

"Yeah, I'm missing my staff," Kwami said.

Rabbit searched her pockets. Her face told Finn that her slingshot had been confiscated, too.

Two huge wooden doors flew open across the room, and a tick-tock man stomped through them.

"ON YOUR FEET. THE MAYOR APPROACHES," the robot barked.

A dark-skinned woman in a pale green military uniform entered. Her outfit looked freshly ironed. Of all the people Finn had seen in the subatomic, she was the cleanest and best dressed.

"SIX CRIMINALS AWAITING JUDGMENT," the robot continued. "ALL ARE GUILTY OF BREAKING THE CURFEW. ONE ENTERED THE CITY AFTER HOURS USING UNLAWFUL TECHNOLOGY. ALL RESISTED ARREST. ALL ATTACKED AND DESTROYED PROPERTY BELONGING TO PROTON. NUMBER TWO WAS DESTROYED. NUMBER EIGHT WAS DESTROYED. TWO OF THE CHILDREN ARE WANTED FELONS. I WILL REPORT TO PROTON?"

"That won't be necessary," the woman said.

"PROTON MUST BE INFORMED."

"I said I will handle this, Number Nine," she snapped. "You are dismissed!"

The robot hesitated for a moment, then turned and stomped back through the doors, closing them behind itself.

The mayor stepped forward. She eyed the group one by one until finally stopping at Kwami. She stared at him for a long time, then slapped him across the face.

"What have you done?" she cried.

"This is not our fault," he said. "We followed the rules."

"If you followed the rules, then she wouldn't be here," the woman said, pointing at Rabbit.

"She has a mind of her own," he said. "Just like her mother."

The woman approached Rabbit. She cupped the girl's chin in her hand and looked into her eyes. Finn wondered if she intended to slap her as well, but instead, the mayor embraced her tight and close.

"No!" Rabbit said, pulling away as if the woman's touch made her sick to her stomach.

"I am your mother," the woman said.

"My mother would never wear that uniform. She would never work for someone like Proton."

"Rabbit, you have to understand—"

"I understand everything I need to," Rabbit interrupted. "You picked your side, and it wasn't the one your family was on."

"You are putting me in an impossible situation," the woman said. "You are only alive because Proton believes I am loyal to him."

"So, what's next? Are you going to make us dis-appear, like Nico's parents? You know the tick-tock men killed him, right?"

This time, the mayor looked like she really was going to slap Rabbit, but she held her temper.

"Follow me," she said, and hurried to a red velvet tapestry. When she pulled it aside, she revealed a se-cret door in the wall. She flung it open and gestured for everyone to enter.

"Shortcut to the dungeon?" Rabbit asked.

"This will lead you out of the city," her mother said.

"You're letting us go?" Rabbit asked. She sounded genuinely surprised.

"Rabbit, I told you there was another side to this story," Kwami said, then turned to his wife. "What will you do? Proton will kill you."

"If you don't go now, you will never leave," she said.

"Come with us," Kwami pleaded.

"I can't," she said. "It's the only way."

"I can't, either," Finn said. "I was told my father is in this palace. I have to find him. The rest of you can go without me. I'll catch up as soon as I can."

"Your father?" the mayor asked.

"He's looking for Asher," Kwami explained.

The woman's face fell.

"Everyone has to stop this!" Lincoln cried. "Every

time he asks about his dad, someone gets weird, or worse, you dance around the answers. Can't you see how important it is to him? Just tell us the truth!"

Before anyone could answer, a round, shiny drone zipped into the room. It circled the group, focusing a number of lenses on them, as if it were trying to get a view from every angle.

"Sharlene, bring our guests to my lab at once," said an odd mechanical voice.

"Of course," the mayor said, bowing her head toward the drone before it disappeared the way it came. She turned to Kwami with panic in her eyes. "Now it's too late."

A tick-tock man burst into the room again.

"You can't just hand us over to him," Kwami said.

"Of course she can, Dad. That's what she does. You didn't think she'd protect us just because we're family, did you?"

Rabbit's mother lowered her eyes so she could avoid their angry scowls and gestured for them to follow the tick-tock man. The robot led them back through the doors into a long hall that passed several archways. The first led to a solarium overflowing with exotic plants and electric butterflies. The second opened onto a small zoo containing strange glowing animals. A third led to a library, its shelves packed tight with books. When they reached the fourth, a simple black door, Sharlene stopped and turned to Rabbit.

"I know you hate me. I did what I had to so that you could escape this city. I don't expect you to understand, but everything I have done for you and your father was to keep you safe. Do not throw away my sacrifices with sarcasm. Keep your mouth shut. Do not antagonize this man. He is not well."

Rabbit shook her head in disgust.

The tick-tock man pushed the door open to reveal a round room cluttered with tables and tools and machinery, much of it Finn guessed was from the far future. The room itself was completely wrapped in bookshelves except for one huge floor-to-ceiling window in the center that looked onto a field of fruit trees. Several ragged workers used ladders to pick the fruit and place it in baskets even though it was still dark outside. Watching the work from the window was a man in a long purple robe. His arms were folded behind his back, and from across the room he was barely more than a silhouette. Sharlene ushered the group to the center of the room, then cleared her throat.

"My lord, the tick-tock men have captured these troublemakers," she said. "I present them now for your rightful judgment and mercy."

The man did not turn around, and for a moment

Finn wondered if he had heard the mayor at all. He kept staring out the window as if the workers were the most fascinating thing he had ever seen. Finally, he spoke.

"Mayor? Do you see that woman climbing the third tree to the right?"

Sharlene stepped closer to the window.

"Yes."

"She is rather careless with the fruit," he said. "I suspect it may bruise if she continues to handle it."

"I will speak to her immediately," Sharlene asked.

"That won't be necessary," the man said. "Tick-tock, arrest her and then go and collect her family. Place them all in the dungeon."

Finn's ears pricked. The man's voice sounded oddly familiar to him, though it was soaked in madness.

"AS YOU WISH, SIR." The robot exited the room.

"List their crimes, Mayor," the man said.

"All six are guilty of trespassing inside Quarkhaven, violating curfew, and living in an illegal settlement. They have conspired with known enemies of the state, created chaos, and caused damage to property. Three tick-tock men were damaged, two of them beyond repair."

"Serious crimes," the man said. "What sort of punishment would you suggest?"

"I would never be so arrogant as to suggest such a thing to you, my lord."

"No, Sharlene. I want your opinion. What kind of punishment do they deserve? After all, we're talking about your husband and your daughter, correct?"

"I . . . my lord, I have served you with loyalty and honor for these many months, protecting you from enemies near and far. I have proven my worth and undying devotion to your kingdom and your throne. I have never asked for anything from you, but today I—"

The man held up his hand to silence her. She glanced at Kwami and Rabbit, but Finn couldn't read what was on her face.

"These crimes are punishable by death," the man said.

"I've got something to say," Finn said. "None of these people would be in trouble if I hadn't dragged them into it. I came to this world looking for my dad, and they were kind enough to help."

The man turned from his window to face him. Finn nearly fell over. He was Asher Foley, the man who had disappeared two years ago, the same man Finn had been looking for all these months.

"Dad?"

"Dude, your dad is the bad guy?" Julep whispered.

Finn ignored her. He ran forward and threw his arms around his father, squeezing him as tightly as he could.

"I thought you abandoned us," he said as tears raced

down his cheeks. "I was so angry, but then I found out that you were here. It's my fault, but now we can take you home. Mom and Kate are going to be so happy. We've missed you so much. We're going to be a family again."

His father did not hug him back. His body was stiff and cold. Finn looked up into his face, recognized his nose and green eyes and his sandy-blond hair, but it was like looking at a complete stranger. Everything about him was wrong. Finn took a step back, confused and horrified.

"Dad? What's wrong?"

"You shouldn't have come here," his father said. "You are interrupting my work. I've created something glorious here in the subatomic, a world I'm rebuilding in my vision. When it is finished, it will be the template for your world."

"Dad? I don't understand."

"Oh, I don't like that name. *Dad.* It's a bit too familiar. Why don't you just call me Proton? Don't look at me like that. You're disappointed, aren't you? You thought you'd come here and have a happy reunion. It's not all bad news. I'm actually very proud of your resourcefulness. I have no idea how you got here, but it appears to have been very clever. Unfortunately, you have brought traitors to my door," the man said, turning his attention to the others. He pointed his finger at Kwami. "Hello, old friend. Nice to see you and your daughter again."

Kwami stepped in front of Rabbit.

"Leave her alone. She's done nothing to hurt you."

"Her existence hurts me. The children of a person's enemies have a bad habit of growing up and seeking revenge. It's in all the books and movies, so the trick is to get rid of them before they get big and strong and decide to take their shot."

He spun around and pointed at Julep.

"Take this one, for example. The people of this world are struggling with the wheel and making fire, but she had a machine that allowed her to fly into my city. Where did she get it? She aligned herself with our dear friend Hawkins. Isn't that correct, young lady?" he demanded, his voice rising to a frantic pitch. "Did you think I wouldn't recognize one of the advanced technologies he stole from me? I suppose he's out there in the grasslands planning to overrun my kingdom! You realize you're going to suffer a punishment that is rightfully his, correct?"

"Dad! She's my friend," Finn begged.

"She's a spy!" Proton said.

"My lord—" Sharlene interrupted, but she didn't get to finish. Proton raised his hand, revealing a silver glove. It turned bright red and shot a blast of hot neon energy at her. The force wrapped around the woman's body like a snake, and she screamed in agony.

"Dad, no!" Finn shouted. "Let her go!"

His father turned to face him. His fists were clenched, his mouth contorted with rage.

"I TOLD YOU MY NAME IS PROTON!" he roared.

The energy that trapped the mayor dissolved. Sharlene collapsed to the floor, groaning and breathing hard. It was obvious she was in immense pain.

"Mayor, please get on your feet," Proton said.

It seemed her fear of him was worse than her agony. She fought to stand.

"Yes, my lord," she said.

"Put them all in a hole," he commanded. "And lock them up tight. Oh, and one more thing: if you ever dare to ask me for another favor, you will find yourself in a dungeon cell all your own."

Sharlene nodded and led them out of the room. Two tick-tock men were waiting in the hall, and they forced the group down a flight of stairs into a dark subterranean level beneath the palace. The walls were thick with mold, and it smelled like rotting meat. They staggered down the dim corridor. Along the way, Finn peeked into the prison cells they passed. Each was full of filthy prisoners, all watching him with desperate, suffering eyes.

"I'm sorry," Julep whispered to him.

"Yeah," Lincoln added.

He was grateful for their words, but too confused by everything to know how to feel. His father had changed into something horrible. The man he remembered from fishing trips and watching old movies and bedtime stories was gone, replaced by a monster. It was as if Asher Foley were dead, but his body was being controlled by something evil.

Sharlene stopped and unlocked a door. When it was opened, the robots forced everyone into a dark room carved out of the bedrock. The floors and walls were damp, and there was little light. Finn couldn't even see the far end of the room.

"I'm sorry I—" said the mayor, but Rabbit interrupted her.

"I never want to see you again," she said, then turned her back on her mother. Kwami put his arm around her shoulders to console her, but she shook him off.

Sharlene looked like her heart was breaking. She closed the cell door, and a second later, a lock turned. Finn could hear her walk back down the tunnel, followed by her metal guards.

"You knew about my father the whole time," Finn said to Kwami.

"I'm sorry, Finn. I didn't know how to tell you. When I found him, he was kind and friendly, always talking about how he had to find a way back to you and his family, but then one day, he changed. It was like he lost his mind."

Finn sat on the floor because he didn't trust his legs to keep him upright anymore. Nothing felt stable or safe. His head was pounding, and he was sure he was going to vomit. Everything was upside down and inside out. What was real? All this time, he'd thought his father was the answer to his troubles. But finding him made everything worse, and he had ignored all the warning signs. His dad had killed people. He sent his hulking robots to terrorize everyone. He controlled this world with fear and madness.

Lincoln and Julep sat down next to him.

"You don't have to say it," Finn said before they could speak. "I dragged you here, and for what? My dad is . . . I don't know what he is. There is nothing you're going to say to me that's going to make me feel any worse, so just save it."

"I was going to say I'm sorry," Lincoln replied. He sat just close enough that their shoulders touched. "I have no idea how you feel, but I imagine it's horrible."

Julep took Finn's hand and squeezed it.

"Me too," she said. "This doesn't make sense."

"If something happens to the two of you, it's all my fault. I was selfish to drag you along with me. I just needed my friends, even if they don't exist anymore.

Every good thing that has happened to me in the last two years is because of the both of you, or rather, them. I still can't get it straight. I'm sorry."

"Shut up, derp," Lincoln said.

"What did you call me?" Finn asked.

"You heard me, derp," Lincoln said.

"Where did you hear that word?" Finn asked.

"Don't know. I just made it up. Listen, I'll admit, when this started I thought you were big box of turds with legs, but you're not so bad. I mean, you're still annoying, but I don't hate you."

"Yeah, and you can't say we're not friends," Julop said. She looked at Lincoln, but he rolled his eyes. She shot him an angry glare, and he laughed. "Aside from being locked in a dungeon by an insane dictator, we've had a pretty good time. It's not a deal breaker for me. Plus, I had a jet pack for a while. That was pretty cool."

"Enough!" Rabbit said. "Finn is not the only one around here who has a parent they can't trust. My mom just locked us in a cell. I lost my best friend in the streets!"

Rabbit pressed herself against the door and looked through the tiny window into the hall. It was as far as she could get from the others.

"I'm sorry about Nico. We're all sorry," Finn said.

"Sorry isn't going to bring him back," she cried.

"We can't start turning on each other," Kwami said. "We need to stay united."

"Finn?" A raspy voice came from the darkest end of the cell. It was followed by a rustling sound. They weren't alone. It didn't come as a surprise. All the cells were packed tight. Finn squinted into the dark and made out the rough outline of a thin, shaggy man in rags. "Is that you or is it my head playing games with me again?"

Finn stood and stepped forward, hoping to get a better look at the prisoner.

"Who are you?"

"You look like him, but you can't be," the man said just before breaking into a wicked coughing fit.

Finn moved closer.

"How do you know me?" Finn asked.

The man snatched Finn's hand and pulled him close.

"You're real."

Frightened, Finn staggered backward, dragging the man with him. Now that he was in the light, Finn gasped. The prisoner looked just like his father, weathered, tired, and hungry, but it was him. His eyes bubbled with tears, and he cried and laughed at the same time.

"You found me," the man said. "How did you find me?"

"Um . . . what's going on?" Lincoln asked.

"I was just about to ask you," Julep said.

"Asher?" Kwami rushed across the room and wrapped the man in a hug. "Asher, you have to explain what's happening. Why are there two of you?"

All the excitement seemed to take a lot out of Asher. Finn and Kwami helped him sit.

"I was just trying to get home," he said.

"I don't understand," Finn said.

"There's a machine that makes copies," he said. "I used it, and I shouldn't have. I have brought all this misery down on the world."

"Is it really you?" Finn asked.

Asher pulled the boy into his arms.

"It's really me, son." He held him close, like he might never let him go. "Proton is a copy of me, and a very bad one, too. I'm the original."

"This is a trick," Rabbit warned. "We saw you upstairs. Now you're down here pretending to be someone else. We're not fools!"

Asher struggled to explain, but it was clear his mind was not well. His mouth opened several times as he choked on words, until he passed out in Finn's arms.

"He looks terrible," Julep said.

"He's exhausted," Kwami said. "It looks like he's been down here a long time."

"Kwami, if you know something you can't hold it

back anymore. I need the truth. Is this my dad or not?" Finn demanded. "And if he is, who is that maniac upstairs?"

Kwami shook his head.

"I think this is your dad," Kwami said. "And I think I understand why this world has been suffering all these months."

"Um, this is probably not the right time to say this, but we have bigger problems than too many Asher Foleys. The sun is about to come up," Julep said. She raised her head and looked out a high window on the wall. A tiny stream of sunlight was shining into the room.

"Why is that a problem?" Lincoln said.

"'Cause when it rises, Quarkhaven is going to war."

22

The tick-tock men were everywhere. Kraven counted fifteen of them, each charging down the roads, blasting lights into every open doorway. They shouted threats of imprisonment and reminders of Proton's lack of mercy for those dumb enough to break his laws. The sky was Kraven's only chance of getting to the palace to rescue Finn Foley. It had the added benefit of giving him an impressive entrance, which he hoped Proton would appreciate. He had never respected a human before, but this world's leader had sparked something close to admiration in the bug.

Unfortunately, try as he might, he could not get off the ground while carrying the infernal robot. Highbeam weighed close to three hundred pounds, so if Kraven wanted to get airborne, he had to get creative.

He hauled the robot's lifeless body onto the roof of one of the shacks, then onto another. The structures weren't that high, but they were the tallest in the entire city, aside from the palace. Once Kraven was ready, he hefted Highbeam onto his shoulders, extended his wings, and started flapping as fiercely as he could. With one fateful step, he hopped off the ledge. It was a miracle he didn't crash to the ground. He was flying!

Joy was an uncomfortable emotion, and he was ashamed for how it made him feel, but no one back on the mother ship had to know. He shook off the strange feeling and pointed himself toward the palace. What would he do when he got there? What would he say to Proton? Naturally, the man would be intimidated by him—humans were terrified of Plague—and the fool would turn Finn Foley over to avoid a conflict. The boy would be in his clutches in no time, and soon Kraven would be back home, with his people.

Unfortunately, just as the palace came into sight, Kraven felt an intense pain that coursed through his entire body. He saw sparks of electricity shooting off his exoskeleton, but had no idea where the energy was coming from. His body was no longer under his control, and he crashed into the ground, tossing Highbeam several yards away.

"UNLAWFUL FLIGHT IS A VIOLATION OF PROTON'S LAW."

He heard the thud of a tick-tock man's foot, but he was unable to stand, talk, or fight. An enormous metal hand scooped him off the ground. The bulky robot was not gentle. It practically yanked out Kraven's wings as it manhandled him. He was helpless and watched the robot snatch Highbeam in his other hand. Moments later the machine was carrying them both toward the palace.

The tick-tock man stomped through the filth of the city until he reached the gleaming palace at the end of the alleyway. It stood four stories high, constructed of brilliant white marble and golden columns. There was a tower on either side and a domed glass ceiling on top. The robot stomped up the stairs to the entrance, pushed open a door, and entered.

Inside was a majestic hallway that soared three stories, lined with purple tapestries and statues of a man in a flowing cape. Despite his discomfort, Kraven was impressed. There were rumors on the mother ship that the admiral's quarters were lavish. Even though Kraven had been promoted to commander, his personal space was dark and small. Kraven swore someday he would be admiral and his quarters would be magnificent. He would let his underlings see it, so they could sulk in their rooms and make themselves sick with envy. He suspected Proton had the same idea.

The tick-tock man marched through the grand hall,

up several flights of stairs, and into a lab. It was messy with electronics scattered across everything. Sitting on the floor, cross-legged, was a pinkskin in a cape. He looked exactly like the statues in the hall, except he was wearing a pair of goggles that magnified the delicate work he was doing on a small white gadget. He poked at its wiring with a tiny screwdriver and was so engrossed he didn't look up when the robot arrived.

"What is it?" he asked.

"ANOTHER CURFEW BREAKER HAS BEEN ARRESTED."

"Why are you bothering me with this? Take them to the mayor," he complained.

"YOUR ORDERS ARE TO BRING YOU ANY UNUSUAL PRISONERS."

Proton set down his gadget and took off his goggles before looking up. When he saw Kraven, his reaction was not what the bug expected. He stood and calmly stepped closer to get a better look at him.

"How does a Plague soldier find its way to the subatomic? And how does he get a Nemethian demo bot as a companion?"

"You know what I am?" Kraven asked.

"My maker lived an unusual life. He encountered many things, though none quite as grotesque as you," Proton said. "I share his memories. I assume you arrived here with Finn Foley and the other Earth children. Are you a traitor to your species, teaming up with humans?"

"How dare you!" Kraven roared. He was feeling stronger. The effects of the shock were wearing off. "No Plague soldier would ever side with a human. Our mother ship hovers over their filthy planet, draining it dry as I speak. We have conquered mankind as easily as we have conquered every world we have ever come across."

"Then why are you here with my son?"

"Your son? You're Ashor Foley?"

"DON'T SAY THAT NAME!" Proton roared. His anger bounced off the glass ceiling and back at Kraven.

"The boy was my prisoner. He rebelled against my people's glorious cause when we arrived on Earth," Kraven said matter-of-factly. "Somehow he escaped our prisons. It is my duty to recapture him, or kill him while trying."

"You have my sympathies. Seems as if dumb courage runs in the Foley family. His father is rotting in a dungeon beneath our feet for the very same crime. So I guess it's safe to assume you and your broken robot were headed toward my palace to steal the boy away from me?"

"I came with respect in hopes of making a deal," Kraven said. "But your crude army of metallic morons shot me out of the sky."

The tick-tock man dropped Highbeam. He clanged hard on the marble floor.

"A deal?" Proton laughed. "What do you have to offer?"

"Finn Foley is the key to returning home," the bug said, ignoring the man's insulting laughter. "Surrender him and I will make the technology available to you. I was told you have been trapped here on this dusty ball of filth for a long time. I assume you might be interested in leaving it."

"Home? You have a way to return to Earth?"

"I do," Kraven said, thinking of it stuffed inside his jacket.

"So why do you need the boy?"

"The machine that brought me here works alongside a technology that is fused to Finn Foley's body. It won't work without him."

Proton nodded. He looked down at the gadget that had absorbed his attention when Kraven arrived.

"I have been hovering over this useless piece of junk for more nights than I can count. My very existence was born from a need to fix it, but despite my superior intellect, I have failed. Your offer comes at a very good time, bug. An invading force is marching on this town as we speak. I could, of course, put it down with little effort, but what's the point? I have done all I can for this world. It has never appreciated my efforts and has fought me at every turn. Now it rises up against me? Me? Well, I will rob it of its chance for revenge and return home, where I can put the things I have learned here to better use."

He set his machine down on a table, picked up a hammer, and smashed it angrily.

"Number Nine, fetch Finn Foley from the hole," he continued.

The robot lumbered out of the room without a word.

Now that they were alone, Kraven eyed the man closely. There was something unsettling about him. Most humans were docile and dumb, but this one . . . he was at war with himself. His voice was a mix of madness and overconfidence. A fool like this would cause problems for the Plague. Setting him loose on the human population might demoralize the pinkskins, but how long before he got tired of tormenting others and turned his attention to the armada?

"I suppose I should start packing," Proton said.

23

With everyone gathered, Julep told the story of how she'd been searching for Finn, Lincoln, and Highbeam when she woke up in the grasslands. She told them about the electric bear, Hawkins, his army of rebels, and his stockpile of futuristic weapons.

"Hawkins's army is huge. They're going to destroy this town, and I suspect the palace is their main target. I think Hawkins can do it, too. The weapons he has are like something in a science fiction movie," she said. "Finn, you wouldn't believe it."

"I believe it. It's our fault," Finn said.

"Us? Huh?" Lincoln asked.

"I haven't told you everything about our lives together," Finn said, taking out Julep's dead phone again. "This thing has pictures of stuff we did in a timeline that probably won't happen now. In that life we were trying to defeat a monster called Paradox, and to do it we sort of stole weapons from the future and stored them here in the subatomic. There's roughly sixty years of criminal behavior in Hawkins's stash."

"That explains a lot," Kwami said. "Asher and I never understood where it all came from or how it got here—even the gadget he found on his jacket. Your dad was sure it was what caused him to shrink. He was obsessed with fixing it so he could get back home."

"The weapons you sent here have ruined everything. They're the reason we suffer," Rabbit said. "It's not like it was a paradise. People struggled. They went hungry and died, and lots of days were hardships, but we didn't have tick-tock men and Proton."

"I'm sorry. I'm sure if Old Man Finn knew the consequences he wouldn't have done it. I mean, I hope he wouldn't have. Honestly, every time I turn around, I'm making a decision that hurts someone else. I did the same thing to you and Julep," he said to Lincoln.

"What are you talking about?" Lincoln said.

"Nothing," Finn said, trying to change the subject.

"No, it's time to talk," Julep said. "You told us that we all used to be best friends, but you changed something in the past and that's why we don't remember you. Everyone else is telling the truth. It's time for you to do the same, Finn Foley."

Finn sighed. They deserved to know what happened.

"Lincoln—I mean, the Lincoln I knew—lived with his father in the same house you live in now. He wasn't a prep-school kid. In fact, he was kicked out of every school in town, and that's how I met him. He was an angry kid, bitter over his mother's death."

"What?" Lincoln cried.

"She died when you were a kid. It was a car accident, so you grew up without her. Well, we were sent on a mission with a pair of time-traveling pajamas and we ended up in your front yard the night she died. So I made sure it didn't happen. Old Man Finn told me not to mess with the past, but what was I supposed to do? You needed her. I knew it would change things. I knew I might create a future where I never met you and we would never be friends. You too, Julep. If it wasn't for Lincoln, I would probably have been too shy to even say hello to you, but I had to take the chance. I just didn't think doing something nice for a friend would change the world so much."

Asher stirred and Finn rushed to his side.

"It wasn't a dream," his dad said.

"No, Dad. I'm here. I'm real."

Finn helped him sit up. It triggered a coughing fit that took a while to get under control.

"Dad, why are there two of you?" Finn asked.

"I was trying to find a way home, but the machine that brought me here was broken," he explained. "I'm not a scientist or an engineer. I didn't know how to fix it or even where to begin. Months passed and I was getting desperate. I missed you and Mom and Kate so much, and I worried you thought I had abandoned you. It was hopeless, but I refused to give up, so I looked through some of the things Kwami and Hawkins found in the grasslands. It was obvious to me that some of the technology came from the future. I've made enough visits there myself as a Time Ranger."

"A what?" Julep asked.

"Let me guess," Lincoln said. "It's a long story."

"If we get out of this alive, it's one you're going to tell me, or else," Julep teased.

"A lot of the machines were completely new to me—the robot, the drones, so much I didn't understand. I took a few things apart, hoping I might stumble on tech that I could borrow for my machine. Unfortunately, I hit a dead end. I was so frustrated and sure I would never get home, and then Kwami and I found the copier."

"The copier?" Julep asked.

"It sat in the back of the pile for months until I finally dragged it out. I think I was intimidated because it was unlike everything else. It had knobs and switches, like an old stereo system. It took me a day to figure out how to turn it on, but when I did, the results were immediate. A beam shot out of it and hit the robot. A moment later, there were two of them."

"You mean the tick-tock men?" Rabbit said.

Asher nodded.

"Kwami told me a little about this," Finn said. "The copy was defective?"

"Yeah, parts of the machine were slightly off. It wasn't serious, but sometimes the second robot would jam up for no reason. We tried it on small things like shoes and chairs. There weren't any problems. We just assumed that the more complicated the thing we wanted to copy, the more problems it would have."

"Naturally, I got curious, too," Kwami said. "Asher lit a fire in me to understand it. I wanted to know how it worked so we started experimenting. We tried bread and fruit and rocks, literally anything we found in the street. The process was fast and worked perfectly until we started messing with the knobs. We found we could adjust the copies to make improvements, like if a can was rusty, the copier would make another that was shiny and new."

"I don't understand what this has to do with Proton," Rabbit said.

"Like I said, I was desperate to get home," Asher explained. "The copier was interesting, but it wasn't helping me get home. Every day that passed felt like a waste of time. I was no closer to getting home, and I cursed myself for not being smart enough to fix the problem. I sank into a depression. I really felt like I was losing my mind. It was then that I got the idea that changed everything."

"You made a copy of yourself!" Finn cried, guessing where his father's story was going.

Asher nodded. There was a terrible shame on his face.

"I needed help, an assistant who was smarter than me. I thought if I could make a genius version of myself, maybe it could fix the gadget and get me home. It was selfish. I didn't think about the repercussions. I was desperate, so I adjusted the controls and zapped myself. A moment later, I was looking at my twin. On the outside he was a perfect copy. He even had the same freckles on his arms. It was amazing. He talked like I did, we liked the same things—it was surreal. And best of all, he was brilliant. He dove into the work. It seemed like the answer to my prayers."

"And then we found the can," Kwami said. "The copy we made of it that was once shiny and new was disintegrating. The copies didn't last."

"That's why Proton is the way he is?" Julep said. "He's falling apart?"

"I went to him as soon as I learned the truth," Asher said. "I was concerned for his health, worried that what we had done might cause him to get sick or even die, but he wouldn't listen. He flew into a rage and accused me of making it all up. He was completely unhinged. Unfortunately, he was the smartest man in the sub-atomic. He took the tick-tock men I'd created, copied a bigger army of them, and put them to work on this palace. I tried to stop him, but he got more and more irrational. Soon he had complete control over the city and the terror began."

"You couldn't have known what was going to happen," Kwami said. "Neither of us did."

"I was fooling around with things I had no business using," Asher said.

Without warning, the door to the cell opened and a tick-tock man marched into the room.

"FINN FOLEY WILL COME WITH ME."

"No!" Asher cried. "Leave my son alone!"

Lincoln and Julep stepped in the robot's way.

"Forget it," Lincoln said, but the robot shoved them aside. Finn was dragged out of the room, and the door slammed shut.

"Leave him alone!" Finn heard his father's pleading all the way down the hall.

24

"**H**ighbeam!" Finn cried when he entered Proton's lab. Somehow he managed to wrench himself free from the tick-tock man and race to his friend's side. The rainbow circle was still spinning on his cracked glass face.

"Hello, son," Proton said.

"Don't call me that. You're not my father. He's in your dungeon and he told me everything! How did Highbeam end up here? What have you done to him?"

"Have it your way, boy."

Kraven stepped from behind a column.

"Let me guess. You two are working together now," Finn said.

"We have mutual interests," Proton said. "My

partner tells me that you are an essential element to getting us all back to Earth."

"I don't know what you're talking about."

"The boy is calling you a liar, bug," Proton said.

Sin Kraven stomped across the room, snatched Finn by the shirt collar, and pulled him off his feet.

"You have tested my patience for too long, human. It is time to accept reality. You have nowhere to run and no friends to save you," the bug shrieked. "Your only choice is to turn on the slide and send us home or I swear—"

"Or what?" Finn said. Any fear he should have felt was gone. He was too tired to be afraid. Now he was just angry.

"Have you ever pulled the wings off an insect? I can do something quite similar to you," Kraven threatened. He tossed Finn and he crashed hard on the stone floor. As he recovered, the Plague soldier pulled the roll of blue tarp from inside his jacket and shook it at Finn. "Turn it on."

At first Finn didn't understand. Why didn't Kraven do it himself, but then it suddenly made sense. The slip-and-slide was fueled partly by the intergalactic lunch-box, and half of it was stuck to Finn's chest. He was the key to going home. He smiled, suddenly understanding how much power he had over the situation.

"Child, your father has been in my dungeon for a

year. I have enjoyed having him as a pet, but I will happily send a tick-tock man down to kill him if you do not turn on that machine," Proton said.

Finn could see the sickness behind the man's eyes. Suddenly, he didn't resemble his dad at all. His father was kind and peaceful and loving. Proton was all hate.

"No," he replied.

"Very well. Number Nine, put an end to Asher Foley," the lunatic raged.

"YES, MY LORD."

"Stop!" Finn cried. "I'll do it. I'll turn on the slide."

"Delay that order, Number Nine," Proton said. "I'd like to give the boy a second chance. See, I'm not terrible. What I want isn't that bad. Send us back to Earth. Have a go at it, boy. I can't wait to see how it works."

Finn couldn't see a way out. Reluctantly, he took the rolled-up tarp from Kraven and spread it flat on the floor. The moment he touched it, he could feel it powering up in his hands. The surface grew slick and wet.

"Fascinating," Proton said. "Now, how do we do this?"

"You run and dive, and the machine does the rest," Kraven explained.

"Excellent. Tick-tock . . . ," Proton said.

Before Kraven could react, the robot had its hands wrapped around his torso. He struggled, but even with his strength he couldn't break free.

"I know what you're going to say. *We had a deal!*" Proton said. "Everyone says that to me. I know you're upset, but one less bug is one less thing I have to conquer on Earth. You understand, don't you? I need you to stay here, but try to think of it as an opportunity. If there is anything left of Quarkhaven after Hawkins and his army attack, feel free to take control and rule it as your own kingdom. Honestly, isn't that kind of great?"

Proton scooped up the slide and turned to his metallic goon. "Take the bug down to the dungeon with the others; then meet me in the dome. We're going to make a thousand copies of you, my friend. It seems we have an infestation of pests to clean out when I return to Earth before we can take control."

"AS YOU WISH." The tick-tock man grabbed Kraven as the bug shouted threats.

"Come along, boy," Proton said as he snatched Finn roughly by the arm. "We have work to do."

"Get away from me!" Finn shouted as he fought to free himself.

"You heard the kid. Keep your mitts to yourself!"

Finn turned and saw Highbeam rise from the floor. The swirling color wheel was gone from his glass face. It was replaced with icons that formed an angry expression.

The tick-tock man holding Kraven tossed him against a wall. The bug smashed hard and tumbled to the floor, unconscious. Then the machine turned its attention to Highbeam.

"YOU ARE BREAKING THE LAWS OF PROTON."

"Actually, I'm breaking your ugly face," Highbeam said. He leaped into the air, pulled back, and threw a punch so hard the bigger machine stumbled backward. Unfortunately, it righted itself almost immediately and socked Highbeam with a punch of its own. Finn's friend crashed against the stone wall, leaving a crater the same shape as his body. Somehow, he survived the attack and got back to his foot.

"Oh, we got a tough guy, huh?" Highbeam said as he cracked the knuckles of his metal hands. "All right, let's get rough. Demo mode!"

His head sank into his chest so that only his eyes could be seen, and a big orange light on his chest flashed a warning. His huge cable arms spun like propellers, and once they were at full speed, Highbeam rushed toward the tick-tock man. They collided in a storm of metal and fists, but Highbeam's arms sliced through its evil torso like butter.

During the tussle, Finn heard a roaring horn drift through the windows.

"ALERT! THE CITY IS UNDER ATTACK!" the tick-tock man said, suddenly turning its attention to the door. Distracted, it couldn't stop Highbeam from cutting it in half, right down the middle.

"Where's the weird guy in the purple cape?" Highbeam asked.

Finn scanned the room. There was no sign of Proton.

"He's headed to his lab to make an army . . . and he took the slip-and-slide with him," Finn said as he rushed to the window. He had a direct view of the entire city. The strange suns of the subatomic were rising over the horizon, and Quarkhaven was soaked in dirty reds and oranges. In the streets below, people were racing toward the main gate. Some of them held spears. Tick-tock men stomped alongside them, but what was amazing was what Finn saw behind the wall. There were thousands of people marching toward the city led by a man on a Plague hoverbike.

"Clearly I missed a lot," Highbeam said as he joined Finn at the window. "What's all the hubbub about?"

"There's a lot to explain. An army is attacking the city. Proton wants to invade and conquer Earth. My friends are in the dungeon and my dad has an evil clone."

"Where do we start? Shouldn't we get the slide first?"

"Proton can't use it without me," Finn said, tapping the device on his chest. "And he knows I need it to get everyone home. I can't stop whatever he's planning right now. We need to save my dad and my friends and we'll face him together."

A rocket screamed across the sky. It slammed into the palace wall and shook the entire building. Dust and pieces of stone came down on Finn's head, but luckily he wasn't hurt.

"The roof is coming down on our heads. Where is the dungeon?" Highbeam asked.

Finn led him back the way he'd come, down the dark hallway and the moldy flight of stairs. When they reached the bottom, he stopped in his tracks.

"What's up, Finn?" Highbeam asked.

Another BOOM! This one sounded like it was right on top of them.

"This dungeon is full of prisoners," Finn said. "We have to free everybody. Hurry!"

They went from cell to cell. There were no keys, so Highbeam broke the locks with a punch, freeing the folks trapped inside. Some were so tired and ragged they couldn't walk, and the other prisoners had to carry them out.

"You have to get out of the city!" Finn shouted. "It's not safe in Quarkhaven."

It was slow, stressful work, and every few moments, the building took another rocket or bomb. Finn could hear the roar of crowds and the familiar sounds of laser guns. He wondered if he and Highbeam would even make it to the cell holding his father and his friends before everything fell down on top of them. Sometimes, when Highbeam opened a door, the prisoners were so terrified by him they cowered in the corners.

"He's not a tick-tock man," Finn explained.

"I happen to be a demolition bot with the full upgrade package, thank you very much!" Highbeam cried, clearly humiliated that he would be mistaken for the "piles of junk on legs," as he called the tick-tocks.

"Keep freeing people," Finn said. "I'll try to get my dad's cell door open."

He ran deeper into the dungeon. Another explosion sent him wobbling and slamming against the wall, but he managed to right himself and keep going. At last, he found the right door. Kwami was on the other side. Panic was all over his face.

"You have to get us out of here, Finn!" he said.

"I'm working on it!" the boy cried as he tried the lock. Like all the others, he needed a key he didn't have. "Highbeam, hurry!"

The robot was too busy opening other doors. If he heard Finn over all the chaos, there was no way of knowing.

"Hawkins is here," Julep said, pushing her way to the window. "He said he plans to burn the city to the ground."

"Where's the slip-and-slide?" Lincoln said, pressing to be seen.

"Proton has it," Finn admitted.

Lincoln looked horrified.

"It's fine. We'll get it back," Finn promised, though he wasn't sure how. "Highbeam, c'mon!"

Someone shoved Finn aside. When he saw who it was, he was stunned.

"Sharlene?" Kwami said.

The woman reached into her pocket and took out a set of keys. Soon the door was open, and everyone poured into the hall. Julep and Lincoln helped Finn's dad walk—he was too weak to do it on his own.

"You have to go," she said.

"What about the other prisoners?" Finn asked.

"I'll free everyone and get them out," she promised.

Another explosion caused a beam to crack. It came down and would have crushed Finn if Highbeam hadn't caught it in his hand.

"You're not going to make it out of here alive," Kwami told his wife.

She took his hand and held it for a moment.

"Let me go out a hero." She kissed him and turned to her daughter. "Someday I hope you'll understand why I did what I did. I love you, Rabbit."

Rabbit hesitated. For the first time since Finn had met her, she wasn't scowling. Now her face was full of regret. She nodded to her mom and gave her a hug.

"I'm not leaving you," she cried.

"Kwami, get her out of here," Sharlene said.

Rabbit's father dragged her away, and everyone followed. Everything was collapsing around them. There was a cave-in that blocked their path, but Highbeam plowed through it. They came out the other side into the grand hall. A broken tick-tock man lay twisted and burning on the floor. Kraven was nowhere to be seen.

"Where do you think the bug went?" Finn asked Highbeam.

"After Proton," he said. "Kraven will want his revenge. You said this Proton is making more robots?"

"He's in the dome," Asher said. "It's the only space in the palace big enough to hold a robot army."

Finn turned to Rabbit and Kwami. "You've done enough. Take as many people as you can and get them out of the city. This is my fight from now on."

"Good luck," Rabbit said.

Kwami shook his hand and turned to Finn's father.

"You were right about your boy. He's something else," he said.

Kwami and Rabbit fled though the throne room and out the golden doors just as another rocket crashed into the palace. It tore off the right side of the building, exposing the outside. It was a miracle no one was hurt.

"This doesn't look good!" Lincoln shouted.

"Just think about it like this, Sidana. Toppling a

dictatorship is going to look amazing on your college application," Julep said.

"That joke hasn't been funny for days," Lincoln said.

"The dome is upstairs," Asher said while Highbeam scooped him up in his arms.

"C'mon!" Finn cried.

They darted up one flight of stairs and then another. At the top, the children pushed open a set of doors, ready to fight Proton if they had to. Their arrival drew the attention of a thousand freshly copied tick-tock men. They turned in unison and stared with their lifeless red eyes.

"TRESPASSERS WILL BE PUNISHED."

"Calm down, tick-tocks," Proton shouted. "It's a party, and the guests of honor have arrived."

25

Kraven was boiling with rage. Humans were supposed to be simple, primitive people, docile even, but the Foley family—they were cold and ruthless. Proton was the most diabolical of the bunch, but he had underestimated Kraven's desire for revenge. The bug intended to kill him, but first he needed a weapon.

The subatomic world was even more backward than Earth. These people were fighting with rocks and sticks, but the invading army outside the city gate was proving to be a different breed. The moment he fled the palace he heard familiar sounds coming from the attack: sonic grenades, laser blasts, advanced-technology weapons. The army had their filthy hands on some very powerful tools, and Kraven was determined to have one for himself. With his wings flapping like thunder, he flew toward the army, ignoring the grogginess from being slugged by the monstrous robot. His vision was blurry and spotty, and he felt like he might fall out of the sky, but hate was a powerful fuel.

As he approached the city gate, Kraven saw Proton's robots fighting a failing battle to keep the invaders out. Thousands and thousands of soldiers, some armed with swords and hammers, were pushing their way through, while others shot off violent and terrible devices. Some of the blows froze the robots in their tracks. Others melted them into puddles of molten steel. Rockets zipped over the city wall, aimed at the palace. Lasers cut through the stone. A huge portion of the wall had already fallen, and the rest was about to come down. Quarkhaven was doomed. Kraven couldn't have cared less. He had a plan of his own. He scanned the invading army and spotted something that would be perfect. A man leading the charge was riding a Plague hoverbike.

Kraven dropped out of the sky and kicked him off the bike with his back leg. Kraven was in the seat before it could even tip over. With a twist of the accelerator, he sped through the fighting. Some of the warriors fell under his bike. When he reached a mob he could not drive through, he pressed a button on the control panel and a wave of sound exploded from the front of his bike, knocking everyone out of his way. Once he got through the gate, he steered toward the palace, pushing the hoverbike's engine to its limit.

"I am Sin Kraven!" he roared. "Commander of the Plague mother ship. And no one makes a fool of me!"

26

"Look, it's the Folcys and their friends," Proton said as he crossed the room. "Congratulations! You managed to rescue your father and your buddies. I presume you emptied out my dungeons, too. Oh, and the big pile of junk walks and talks now?"

"Watch your mouth, punk," Highbeam said.

"My apologies. I'm smart enough to know I don't want to go head-to-head with you. This gang has got luck on its side, doesn't it? Oh, Asher, don't interrupt me. You know how I hate that. Hear me out. I have had an excellent idea. The way I see it, we all want the same thing: to get off this miserable world. Am I right? I mean, that's why I was created, after all, and I've done my best to make that happen. Of course, I have loftier goals, as well, like conquering

Earth, but if we boil it all down, getting back home is what's important. But here's the problem—the Plague. You want them to go away. I want them to go away. It's very hard to take over a planet someone has just taken over, so here's what I propose. Let's turn on your magic slide. I'll send my robots to the mother ship to do what they do best, and when the dust is settled and the Plague are on their knees, well, we'll figure out the rest later. What do you say, son of mine?"

Finn bristled. Proton's eyes were spinning in his head. He looked as if he might break into hysterical laughter, but hearing the man call him "son" still made him angry. Unfortunately, this lunatic had a point. Finn looked at his friends, his father, and finally Highbeam. An army of tick-tock men *might* have a chance at destroying the bugs.

"You're not actually considering this, are you?" Lincoln said, much to Finn's surprise.

"Maybe. You've been wanting to go home since we left. Now's our chance," Finn said.

"I don't see the bright side of swapping bugs for robots. I hate this place, but I'm not going to let Evil Dad set one foot on planet Earth," Lincoln said.

"I agree," Julep said. "I'd rather be stuck here. Earth has enough trouble. Besides, if Hawkins and his army don't take this idiot down, then I'll start my own rebellion to finish the job. The Mongoose has plenty more trouble to make."

Finn turned to Highbeam.

"I always have your back, little man, but I vote for keeping this psycho in the subatomic."

Asher rested his hand on his son's shoulder.

"You know what the right thing is," he said.

A series of rockets hit the street outside. The noise nearly drowned out the army that was approaching.

"It's now or never, boy," Proton said.

Finn shook his head.

"No deal."

"Isn't it just like a Foley to do it the hard way on purpose? All right, plan B, then," Proton said. He raised the hand that wore the silver glove and fired an energy blast at Finn's father. It hit him in the gut, and Asher collapsed. Finn and the others encircled him.

"Dad! I'm sorry," Finn said while tears ran down his face.

Asher couldn't speak. He clenched Finn's hand and squeezed it tightly.

"Now, let's think about this," Proton said. "Daddy's hurt, but if you get him to a doctor, he might survive. I'll leave that decision up to you, though I'd hate to have to hurt your friends next. Turn on the slide and take us all home, or be stubborn and let the people you love die on a strange world in the middle of a violent uprising."

Asher's eyes said no, but Finn was out of options.

"You win," Finn said to Proton. He took the slip-and-slide from the villain and unfurled it so it lay flat on the floor. The surface flooded with water.

"What a strange device. So you just run and slide, like a kids' backyard toy? Very well. Tick-tock men, let's go for a ride!" Proton shouted, and a dozen robots dove and slid down the tarp, followed by more and more and more. Unfortunately, they didn't shrink. In fact, they got bigger and bigger the closer they got to the end of the slide. Even more bizarre was that the slide itself was growing, too. The larger it got, the more robots could leap onto it. Proton was ecstatic. "Go! Go! Go!"

"Uh-oh," Lincoln said, pointing to the tarp. The slide was filling the room. It knocked out one of the dome's glass walls, unrolling down the side of the palace. The other end did the same and almost forced Finn and his group out the window.

"We better get out of here!" Highbeam shouted.

"C'mon!" Lincoln shouted, and he dove onto the gigantic wet surface, along with the last of the tick-tock men. Julep was next, followed closely by Highbeam and Asher. Finn was ready to be next when Proton leaped in front of him.

"I don't think so, boy!" he roared. His hands went

around Finn's neck and he squeezed. Finn couldn't breathe and couldn't break free. Proton was going to kill him. "I've seen how destiny helps you out. I can't let you ruin any more of my plans."

Finn's vision got spotty. His head was spinning. He clutched at Proton's hands, hoping to free himself, but the man was too strong.

"It's over," Proton shouted.

Without warning, Finn heard glass breaking and the sound of a Plague hoverbike. The bike flew into the room and slammed into Proton, causing him to fly forward and hit the slide. The bike crashed on it, as well. As Finn struggled to breathe, he realized Sin Kraven was getting bigger and bigger, breaking through the top of the dome. The bug reached for Finn, trying to pluck him off the floor, but Finn scurried backward and accidentally tumbled out the window.

By some miracle, Finn's hand caught the ledge. With his feet kicking in midair, he hung over Quarkhaven, and watched the slip-and-slide roll over it street by street. It knocked down buildings and the remainder of the city wall. Desperate, Finn tried to climb back up, but more of the slide fell out of the window and knocked him loose. He fell, certain he was going to die, until he realized his pants and shirt were soaking wet. He was skidding down the slide. In a flash his body quadrupled in size, then did it again. In no time he was practically as tall as the palace itself. His body weight leaned against the structure and it collapsed beneath him. He wondered if he might get so big that he crushed the entire planet, but then a hole, swirling with colors, appeared. It was pulling him inside. He was going home.

27

The first thing Finn understood when he woke up was that the air around him was hot and humid. The second thing he understood was that he was on the Plague mother ship again. The third thing he understood was that he was lying on his back in the middle of a raging battle.

He sat up and saw a thousand locusts fighting a thousand tick-tock men. Kraven was in the middle of the battle. He drove his hoverbike straight at the machines, firing rockets and lasers. His attacks did as much damage to the robots as they did to the surrounding room.

"Destroy this ship!" Proton shouted at his army. Finn looked up and found the man standing next to him. At his feet was the slip-and-slide. Carefully, Finn reached for it, but once he had it in his hand, Proton snatched him by the wrist and yanked him to his feet. The villain's face was pale and sweaty. His skin was covered in what looked like black dust, but it wasn't dirt. It was his face, cracking into tiny pieces. The copy was coming apart.

"You're dying," he gasped.

"Ridiculous!" he cried, but when he spotted the damage on his hands, he let Finn fall back to the ground. Proton tried to brush off the dust. Finn watched the particles swirl in the air. The more he wiped away, the less of him there was. "What's happening?"

At that moment, Kraven appeared. He slugged Proton and the man fell to the floor. While they we fought, Finn scooped up the slip-and-slide and raced through a doorway. He ran as hard and fast as he could, but he could hear Proton and Kraven chasing him, each wanting to end his life for a different reason.

"Leave me be, bug! He's getting away!" Proton shouted.

"I'll kill you and then the boy!" Kraven cried.

Finn didn't slow down to watch who was going to win the fight. He called out for Highbeam, hoping he and his father were nearby. When he didn't get a response, he called for Lincoln and Julep. No one replied, so he kept running aimlessly. The mother ship was dark and gigantic. He realized he could get lost and never be found.

An alarm wailed overhead and an announcement was made in the Plague's horrible clicking and screeching language. He didn't need to understand to know they were sounding an emergency siren. Were they beating back the tick-tock men or were they losing to the machines? He heard footsteps and caught a glimpse of a group of armed bugs racing his way. He slipped through a door, hoping he hadn't been seen. Once inside, he waited for the soldiers to pass.

It gave him a moment to catch his breath and think. He had to find the others and then Pre'at. She might have something that could help his dad's wound, and hopefully she'd have a weapon in case the tick-tock men took over the ship. But where was he supposed to look?

He turned to eyeball the room, hoping it might have something in it he could use, and the sweat froze on his forehead. Six Plague soldiers were watching him from their seats at a massive control panel. He had stumbled into the ship's bridge.

"Sorry! I thought this was the bathroom," he said, then turned and raced back into the hall.

"Stop him!"

He ran down the hall, turning this way and that, not

knowing where he was going and hoping his path was just as confusing to anyone chasing him. He turned a corner and slammed face-first into Julep.

"Finn Foley!" she cried.

"Sorry." He got to his feet. He helped her stand and couldn't stop himself from laughing.

"What's so funny?" she said as she put her glasses back on.

"This is how I met you the first time," he said. "I almost killed us both."

"It's a lousy way to make a friend. Have you seen the others?"

"No," Finn said. "But Proton and Kraven are chasing me, and I just alerted the command center that we're here. So things aren't going too well on my end. We have to find my dad. He needs a doctor."

"C'mon," she said, pointing him back down another hallway. "Let's keep looking."

Together they sped along, shouting for their friends. They looked into empty labs and closets but found nothing. Finally, they pushed through a door and found themselves on the catwalk above the ship's engines. Far below, they heard banging and crashing and a massive explosion.

"I think the tick-tock men found the engine room," Julep said.

"Fine with me. Let's go to Pre'at!" Finn shouted.

The duo scurried up the ladder that led to the ventilation shafts, the same ones they'd used not so long ago. Together they crawled along on their hands and knees, hoping they were making the same turns they had the first time. They heard more alarms, and whenever they came across air slits, they saw bugs racing up and down the halls. Some of them were in a panic.

"He's doing it," Julep said. "Proton is taking over this ship."

"It might not matter," Finn said. "He's dying. I don't think he'll live much longer."

"It's only going to make him more desperate," Julep said.

Finn shuddered. The man was already a maniac.

"Wait! Is this it?" Julep said, peering through a vent. Finn got beside her to take a look for himself. Below was Pre'at's lab. The Alcherian scientist was below, busy at work.

Finn opened the shaft door, lowered himself, and dropped to the floor. Julep was right behind him. To their surprise, Highbeam, Lincoln, and Finn's father were already there. His dad was lying on a table, and Pre'at was using a humming device to scan his belly.

"We found you!" Finn cheered.

"What in heavens is happening?" Pre'at asked.

"Proton," Finn said.

"Is that a person?" she asked.

"I'll explain later. Please help my dad," he begged.

"Of course I can. I'm a genius," she replied. She injected something into Asher's left arm, then waved a machine that lit up his wound with blue light. Finn watched as his skin slowly began to heal itself. After a few seconds, she tossed the machine aside. "He'll survive. Now, we need to focus on getting off this ship."

The door flew open and Kraven fell in with Proton's hands wrapped around his neck. The two fought bitterly, crashing around the room, shouting threats at one another. Finn pulled Julep to safety and joined the others circling his father.

There was another massive explosion and the ship lurched, turning on its side. Everyone tumbled over each other, including Kraven and Proton. They crashed against the wall, but it didn't stop their battle.

"Is there an escape shuttle or something we can take?" Julep asked.

"How would I know?" Pre'at said. "I'm a prisoner. They didn't exactly give me a tour."

"There are pods," Highbeam said. "But they are so far from here we'd never make it. What about this slide? Can we adapt it to get us home?"

"That's not how it works," Pre'at said.

"Can we take it apart?" Finn asked.

"You want the lunchbox, don't you?" Pre'at asked.

Finn nodded.

Pre'at took the slide from Finn and lumbered over to her work desk. It wasn't easy, but she managed. She spread it out as best she could, then pressed a button on the tabletop. Magically, the lunchbox rose out of the plastic, as did Asher's lasso. Finn snatched them both, feeling the incredible power. He focused on his back-yard, and a wormhole appeared.

"Highbeam, help my dad!" he shouted. "Lincoln, Julep, Pre'at—let's go."

Everyone hurried as fast as they could and vanished before his eyes. He was about to jump in himself when he heard the hum of a sonic blaster.

"You aren't leaving without me, are you?" Proton said. Kraven and Proton had stopped their fighting. They stood shoulder to shoulder behind him.

Finn held up his hands.

"It seemed like the fair thing to do was to stop our brawl long enough to kill you," Kraven said.

"What's the matter? Does it make you angry that a little boy beat you again, Kraven? Even with the help of this bad copy of my dad, you still couldn't stop me, and now your ship, your people, and all his tick-tock men are going down for good."

Proton fired the weapon just as the ship lurched again, sending everything topsy-turvy. Finn fell and slid backward. He had to laugh. His wormhole was waiting behind him.

"You two deserve each other," he said as he fell into the stars. The whirlpool closed behind him and re-opened, spitting him out on his front lawn.

The entire neighborhood was outside, staring up at the mother ship, which was on fire and spinning.

The back door opened and Finn's mom and sister raced out. They wrapped Finn in a hug and showered him with kisses.

"We were panicked," Mom said.

"Don't ever disappear on us again," Kate said. "Seriously!"

"Sloan? Kate?"

Finn's father put his hand on his wife's shoulder. She turned around and looked at him. At first, it seemed as if she didn't recognize him.

"I brought him home," Finn said. "I told you I would."

"Asher!" she cried.

"What is going on?" Kate said. She started to cry until he pulled her and Mom into a hug.

"I'm home. I'm home," he said.

"Um, I know this is a very touching moment, but I'd like to point out that the giant spaceship above us is out of control and about to fall on top of the town," Highbeam said. "So can we focus?"

Finn handed his father his lasso.

"Dad, you can fix this, right? You're a Time Ranger. You can go back and stop everything," Finn said.

"Son, I am too weak," Asher said. Despite Pre'at's treatment, he still looked thin and gray.

"You still have the lunchbox," Pre'at said. "Send the ship somewhere else."

"I don't think I can make a wormhole that big," he confessed.

"C'mon, you said that when the three of us are together anything is possible," Julep said, reaching for his hand.

"She's right, Foley," Lincoln said. "You talked a lot about how amazing we are together. It's time to prove it."

Finn stared up at the mother ship. It was massive. Then he looked at the unicorn lunchbox. He had used it to reach the farthest corners of space, but this was totally different. Unfortunately, he didn't have a choice. He and the lunchbox were their only chance. He closed his eyes and scanned through the countless corners of space, the uncharted worlds and dead stars. He saw trillions of aliens hundreds and thousands of light-years away. None of them were right. What he needed was the same place he had sent the Plague before— a place so far from everything it was literally nowhere. And then it appeared in his mind.

"All right, let's see what you've got," he whispered to himself.

The lunchbox shook the ground. All around he heard windows breaking and car alarms blaring. It felt as if he were standing at the center of an earthquake. He heard the zipper open on the lunchbox and a bolt of lightning flew out that cracked a telephone pole in two. The thunder that followed knocked a car on its side.

"Oh boy!" Kate shouted.

"Is this safe?" his mother cried.

Finn held the lunchbox over his head so the whirlpool would form above him. When he looked up, he was happy to see it was enormous, almost the size of the whole block, but it wasn't nearly large enough for the entire ship falling on top of them.

"Think bigger, little man!" Highbeam shouted.

"I am," Finn said, bearing down on his thoughts. *Come on. You can do better than that. Make it bigger. Save the town. Save the people you love.*

"It's growing, Finn Foley. You're doing it," Julep whispered into his ear. She was next to him, holding his hand. It made him nervous and happy at the same time.

"Son, you can do this," his father said.

"We believe in you," his mother said.

"Don't screw it up!" Kate cried.

"Kate!" Mom cried.

The hole got bigger and bigger. The sound of the ship falling from the sky was a whistle that grew louder by the second.

"Little man, it's now or never," Highbeam said.

Finn's head felt like it was cracking in two. He nearly collapsed. Lincoln stepped close to hold him up.

"It hurts!" he cried. "I can't do it."

"You can do it, boy!" Pre'at shouted.

And then Finn heard Lincoln break into song.

"Oh, I am the very model of a modern major general. I've information vegetable, animal, and mineral. I know the kings of England and I quote the fights historical, from Marathon to Waterloo in order categorical—"

"What are you doing?" Finn cried.

"I sing musicals when I'm stressed out!" Lincoln said. "It's from *The Pirates of Penzance*. It's a classic. Is it helping?"

Finn shook his head.

"Sorry, derp," he said.

"You called me a derp," he said. Finn's heart filled with happiness. Maybe this boy wasn't his Lincoln, but he was close enough.

"Finn, you're doing it!" his dad crowed.

Finn looked up. The whirlpool was enormous. It seemed to stretch across Cold Spring, from Bear Mountain nearly all the way to Garrison. And not a moment too soon. The tip of the mother ship crossed its barrier and disappeared slowly but surely into the void, until there was nothing left of it at all. And no sooner than it arrived, the wormhole vanished.

A shrieking pain stabbed Finn's brain, and he fell to the ground.

In the morning, Finn woke to find his dad sitting on the edge of his bed. He looked rested, and there was a glow to his skin again. He wore his pajamas, and there was gauze wrapped tightly around his abdomen.

"You weren't here all night, were you?" Finn asked.

"Son, you've been sleeping for three days."

Finn sat up. "How are you?" he asked.

"Better," said his father. "It's going to be a little while until I'm one hundred percent, but it's very good to be home. You mom has been overfeeding me, and your sister is keeping me busy with a show she loves called *Unicorn Magic*."

"Oh, that's not going to make you feel better."

"Pre'at's downstairs and a little eager to go. We had to hide her in the garage so the neighbors wouldn't spot her, and she is not happy. If you're up to it, do you think you could preheat that lunchbox and take her home?"

He dropped Pre'at and Highbeam off on Nemeth. Within minutes of their arrival, Highbeam's twenty-five robot children raced into the room and swarmed their father. Dax Dargon was with them. She was as excited as the kids.

"The team is back in business, big guy," Dax said to her partner. "Dax Dargon and her sidekick, Highbeam Silverman!"

"I am not your sidekick," the robot grumbled. He bent down so she could kiss his digital face, then turned to Finn.

"I'm not saying goodbye to you, kid. You have a lunchbox that will take you anywhere you want, and I expect you to come and visit me. Isn't that right, kids? Don't you want to spend time with your uncle Finn?"

The robot children cheered.

"Promise," Finn said with a smile. "So what are you going to do now that there's no Plague to fight?"

"Nemeth could probably use a demo bot. Lots of re-building to do around here."

"You're going to give up being a spy?" Dax cried.

"Absolutely," Highbeam said. "I need a vacation."

"Pre'at, take care of yourself," Finn said to the scientist.

"Naturally," she replied. "One thing an Alcherian does is look after her own best interests. I'm going into business for myself selling slip-and-slides."

"To send people to the subatomic?" Finn asked.

"No, as a toy. Kids will love it. I'm going to be very, very rich," she said.

Finn opened another wormhole, waved goodbye to his friends, and went home. His dad was waiting for him in the hammock.

"Come here, buddy," Asher said. "Are you too old to hang out with your dad?"

"Never," Finn said, and he crawled in next to him. They lay there the entire afternoon, telling stories and talking about friends, how to make them, and how to keep them.

28

Finn left several message with Lincoln and Julep, but neither responded. Days passed, and Finn wondered if maybe the growing connection he had felt had just been his imagination. Maybe he'd lost his best friends again.

One night, a week after the Plague was gone, he found a cool spot in the backyard to lie down, and he wrapped his hands behind his head to gaze up at the night sky. The stars were out in all their glory, blowing up the Cold Spring sky like fireworks. It was nice to see it without the mother ship blocking the view, even if he still had a hard time believing that normalcy had finally returned to the world.

"What are you doing?" Kate said. His sister stood over him, staring down at him like he was nuts.

"Nothing, which is exactly what I want to do."

"Come watch *Unicorn Magic* with me," she pleaded. "Fireball is going to try to win the Unicorn Cape. It's a very big episode."

"Maybe later," he said. "Why don't you skip it tonight and hang out with me?"

"Skip it?" she cried, but after a moment she got down on her hands and knees and nestled into a spot right beside him. She kicked off her shoes and let blades of grass slide between her toes. When a lightning bug flew past, she snatched it in her hand, but then let it go.

"I missed you," he said.

"I missed you, too," she replied.

"What's this all about?" Mom said when she suddenly appeared beside them. She didn't wait for an answer. She lay down on the lawn and trained her eyes on the sky.

"It's really beautiful tonight," she said. "I'm glad we're all together."

"I am, too, Mom," Finn said. "Where's Dad?"

"Am I missing something?" Asher said as he stepped out the back door. He was still a little careful with himself, but every day he got stronger. Mom let him keep his scraggly beard for a day, then personally got the scissors out and cut it off herself. He was gaining weight, and the light in his eyes had returned. He was almost back to his old self.

"Now that we're all together," Mom said, "I think we need to make a deal. If anyone in this family is part of a secret club or society that involves space travel, time machines, or anything like that, it's time to confess."

Dad laughed. "I knew this conversation was coming. I can safely say that at this moment, I am not part of any intergalactic club or organization."

Finn shook his head. "Nope. In fact, I don't have any friends at all."

"Don't look at me," Kate said. "Nothing exciting ever happens in my life."

"Not true," Finn said. "You are a member of the Sisterhood of the Bloody Hoof."

"The what?"

"It's a unicorn thing," Finn admitted. "They think very highly of you. I heard they even sing songs about your bravery."

"More of this other-timeline silliness?" Kate said. "Why is the club called the Bloody Hoof? I think something like the Cornies would be much better. Get it? Uni-cornies?"

"You don't want to know why it's called the Bloody Hoof," Finn said. "Oh, and Mom is actually the world's most famous librarian in the distant future."

"I always wanted to be a librarian," Mom replied.

"There's still time," Dad said. "There's always time."

"This is the weirdest family I know," someone said

from behind them. Finn looked up to see Lincoln and Julep approaching. She was wearing a new backpack and it appeared to be stuffed full.

"Look, Finn. It's your friends," Mom said. She was a little too excited. Apparently, the Finn she knew was a bit of a loner.

"Let's give them some space," Dad said. He got to his feet and helped his wife do the same. Together they coaxed Kate, who complained bitterly that she was never allowed to be part of anything.

"What are you two doing here?" Finn asked. "I sort of thought you guys were done with me."

"I would have called, but I've been grounded," Julep said. "Mom and Dad found out I was the Mongoose. My days as a rebel leader are officially over."

"I needed some time to think," Lincoln said.

"Yeah?"

"Yeah," he answered. "So here's what I have to say: It's never going to be cool that you dragged me off to another world where I could have died."

"Never going to be cool," Finn echoed. "Won't happen again."

"But I get that you had experiences with Julep and me that we don't remember. I realize you were used to me jumping into your adventures without worrying I'd say no."

"Again, I think the wild adventures are over," Finn said.

"Let's not be too hasty," Julep said. "You showed me things I had only imagined might be possible. I got my phone charged, and the pictures are insane. I'm grateful. I want more!"

"Before you say anything else, wait here," Finn told Lincoln. He leaped to his feet and hurried into the house. A moment later he came back outside with a box he put into Lincoln's hand.

"What's this?"

"It's a thank-you," Finn said. "I didn't deserve my Lincoln's friendship. I don't deserve yours, but I'd like to earn it. This is my way of saying as much. I hope you like it. You were right. It wasn't easy to get one."

Lincoln opened the box. Inside was a green blazer with a gold patch on the lapel.

"Derp," Lincoln said. He took it out of the box and slipped it on. "It fits."

"What do you say, Lincoln Sidana?" Julep prodded.

"Foley, you're selfish and obsessive and not super smart," Lincoln said.

"Sidana!" Julep cried. Her Southern accent was thicker than ever.

"But the truth is, I'm sort of the same, so since you don't have any friends and I don't have any, I thought maybe . . . do you guys want to come over tomorrow? I have a pool, and—"

"Cannonball contest!" Finn cheered.

"How did you know my dad and I do that?" Lincoln said. "Oh, yeah."

"You two can jump in the pool like idiots all you want. I think I'm going to sit in a lounge chair and catch up on some reading," Julep said, patting her backpack.

"All right, I've got French homework. I gotta run," Lincoln said.

"There's no school!" Julep cried.

"There will be, and you two dummies are going to be way beind."

The kids waved their goodbyes and disappeared into the night.

Finn looked up at the sky once more. He had one last thing to do to make everything right.

"Kate! Bring the lunchbox!"

His sister raced outside with her pink lunchbox in hand.

"What's up? Where are we going?"

"Want to see some real unicorn magic?" he asked as he took the lunchbox from her. The world rumbled beneath their feet as the box bounced around in his hand.

"Seriously?" she cried.

"Seriously!"

Finn focused his mind on the unicorn home world.

He could see its familiar pink sky, and the cotton candy clouds, and the rainbows that poured down on the herds grazing in the fields. The wormhole that would lead them there appeared just as the lunchbox popped open.

"Just a warning. You might not like everything you learn about them," Finn continued.

"What are you keeping from me about unicorns?" Kate demanded as she took her brother's hand.

"Well, they're a lot more bloodthirsty than you might think," he said, and together the Foley siblings rocketed through space.

THE END . . . FOR NOW

Acknowledgments

Writing a book is not a solitary occupation. Lots of people helped me make this one, and to them I offer a humble thank-you. First and foremost, my editor, the legendary Wendy Loggia at Delacorte Press, as well as her staff and the entire team that made the Finniverse an out-of-this-world experience.

Much thanks goes to Alison Fargis, agent extraordinaire, and everyone at Stonesong. You've made a lot of things come true for me.

My dear friend Joe Deasy, who lets me ramble on the phone and read him endless passages, and who gives me excellent advice. I couldn't write these stories without you.

Kirsten Miller, who laughs at all my jokes. Thank you.

And to every teacher, librarian, media specialist, bookseller, and kid who found my work and loved it. Thank you. Thank you. Thank you. But most of all, Finn. You are totally out of this world.

GET READY TO BE SUCKED INTO THE FINNIVERSE!

From the *New York Times* bestselling author of the Sisters Grimm and NERDS series comes an action-packed series with aliens, robots, and kids saving the world!

About the Author

Michael Buckley lives in a part of New York known for evil robot attacks. Luckily, his son, Finn, and their magical wonder dog, Friday, are at his side. Together, they defend the peaceful and simple people of Brooklyn from the metallic, brain-eating horde. Somehow, during all the fires and chaos, Michael found time to write twenty books. They include the Sisters Grimm series and the NERDS series. You might like them. A lot of people suffered while he wrote them. It was time he should have dedicated to fighting the robots.

Do you have more questions? Do you have tips on fighting evil robots? Take a peek at the author's website and his Instagram page.

michaelbuckleywrites.com
@whatsupbuckley